'Are you oka concern.

'Fine,' she moaned
yoga!'

'Are you having a contraction?' He was assessing her; not wanting to just dive in and place his hand on her stomach, he thought he ought to introduce himself first. 'I'm Ben. I'm a doctor.'

'And I'm Celeste...' She blew out a breath and then slowly unfolded. 'And I'm not having a contraction; it's a stitch.'

'You're sure?' he pressed.

'Quite sure!'

He was suddenly slammed back into the past again—just as he was almost every day and every night, not all the time now, but surely, given that it was nearly four years on, *too* many times.

'So long as you're okay,' he clipped, and went to go.

But suddenly she was holding her swollen stomach with both hands, and blowing out a long, slow breath.

'That,' sa

Carol Marinelli recently filled in a form where she was asked for her job title, and was thrilled, after all these years, to be able to put down her answer as 'writer'. Then it asked what Carol did for relaxation and, after chewing her pen for a moment, Carol put down the truth—'writing'. The third question asked—'What are your hobbies?' Well, not wanting to look obsessed or, worse still, boring, she crossed the fingers on her free hand and answered 'swimming and tennis'. But, given that the chlorine in the pool does terrible things to her highlights, and the closest she's got to a tennis racket in the last couple of years is watching the Australian Open, I'm sure you can guess the real answer!

Recent books by the same author:

Mills & Boon® Medical™ Romance

SECRET SHEIKH, SECRET BABY
ENGLISH DOCTOR, ITALIAN BRIDE

Carol also writes for
Mills & Boon® Modern™ Romance!
Look out for her next sizzling story
WEDLOCKED: BANISHED SHEIKH,
UNTOUCHED QUEEN
coming next month
from Mills & Boon® Modern™ Romance

ONE TINY MIRACLE...

BY
CAROL MARINELLI

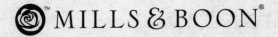

First published in Great Britain 2009
Paperback edition 2010
Harlequin Mills & Boon Limited,
Eton House, 18-24 Paradise Road, Richmond, Surrey TW9 1SR

© Carol Marinelli 2009

ISBN: 978 0 263 87670 3

Printed and bound in Spain
by Litografia Rosés, S.A., Barcelona

ONE TINY MIRACLE…

CHAPTER ONE

A NEW DAY.

A new start.

Another one.

Walking along the beach, Ben Richardson was head down and too deep in thought to really notice the glorious pink sky over the smooth waters of Port Phillip Bay. He had been accepted for a position as Emergency Registrar at Melbourne's Bay View Hospital and would be there in a couple of hours to start his first day, only there were no first-day jitters as he made his way along the beach— after all, he'd had plenty new starts before.

This would be his fourth job in the three years since Jennifer's death…no, it was nearly four years now. The anniversary was coming up soon and Ben was dreading it. Trying and failing not to think about it, trying and failing not to constantly think how life should be, had *they* lived. Had he stayed put at Melbourne Central, had life not changed so dramatically for him, he'd have been starting to apply for consultant positions now. But staying there hadn't been an option—there were just too many memories there for him. After six months of trying, Ben had realised that he couldn't keep working in the same place that he had once worked with his wife and had accepted, after some soul-searching, that things would never be the same again, could never be the same again. So he had moved on to Sydney—which had felt right for a while, but after eighteen months, well, that restless feeling had started again and he'd moved on to another Sydney hospital. Only it had been the same tune, just a different song. The place was great, the people too…

But it just didn't work without Jen.

So now he had returned to Melbourne, but on the out-skirts this time, and it was good to be back closer to his family and amongst old friends again.

No, he wasn't nervous about this new start—the difference was that this time he was looking forward to it, ready for it, excited even by the prospect of finally moving on.

It was time.

He had decided to live by the beach and take brisk walks or jog each morning…except on day three after moving in he'd already pressed the snooze button on his alarm a few times!

Ben picked up speed, even broke into a jog, his large, muscular frame belying his deftness, and all too soon he reached his destination—the house that he had had his eye on for a couple of weeks now.

While working through his notice in Sydney, Ben had made the trip down to find a home close to the hospital. Looking online, speaking on the phone with real-estate agents, he had found several prospects to view over the weekend, determined to secure a home before he started his new job—deciding that maybe if he owned a property then he'd be more inclined to settle for longer.

The real-estate agent had been showing him a typical bachelor apartment, a new development along the beach, with gorgeous bay and City views. It was bright and airy and had all mod cons with the bonus of a huge balcony which would be nice when he had friends or family over. It had everything, really, and Ben had come close to purchasing it that day, but, standing on the balcony as the agent sorted out the documents, Ben had seen the house next door. An older house, it jutted out a touch further onto the beach than the apartment block. The garden, which had direct beach access, was an over-grown green oasis compared to the swish decking and clear-walled balcony that he'd stood on.

Instead of looking at the glorious beach, Ben had found himself gazing into his potential new neighbour's garden. A huge willow tree shaded most of it, there was a slide and swing and a trampoline, but what had really caught Ben's eye had been the boat parked along the side of the house—a man in his forties had been hosing it down and he had looked up and waved as they'd stepped out onto the balcony and Ben had given a quick nod back, only realising then that the man had actually been waving to the real-estate agent instead of himself.

'I'll be with you shortly, Doug,' the agent called, then took a seat at the well-positioned glass table, sorting out brochures and papers and finally locating the contract.

'Is it on the market, then?' Ben asked.

'Sorry?'

'The house next door—is it for sale?'

'Not yet,' the agent said with a noncommittal smile. 'Have a seat, Dr Richardson, and we'll go through the small print.'

'But is it coming onto the market?' Ben persisted.

'Perhaps. Though, really, it has none of the specifications you outlined. That house needs a lot of work, it still has the original kitchen and the garden's a jungle…' Only Ben wasn't listening and the real-estate agent suddenly had that horrible sinking feeling that he was losing his grip on his certain sale. 'The apartment complex is maintained, regularly serviced, there's the gym and lap pool for tenants,' he pointed out, pushing what he assumed were the benefits of living here for this tall, rugged-looking bear of a single guy, with the title of doctor. He had been so sure that low maintenance was the key to this sale.

He was wrong.

Ben was fast realising that high maintenance would be fantastic!

This was a garden and a house he could lose himself in, what with house repairs and oiling decking. And how about a boat…? How much better to fill up his limited spare time renovating a house or out on a boat on the bay than to be confined to modern, sleek lines of the apartment or burning off his endless energy in a lap pool? For the first time in a very long time, Ben found himself interested in something that wasn't work, and, staring at the house, he could almost glimpse a future, a real future… So, instead of closing the deal and moving into the plush apartment complex, to the agent's obvious annoyance, Ben took a gamble, put his furniture into storage and rented one of the cheap furnished units at the other end of the street, prepared to sit it out till the house came on the market.

It was win-win really, Ben thought this morning as he walked along the beach access path to the front of the house. In that short space of time, the bottom had fallen out of the housing market and the developers were having trouble selling the luxury apartments. Already the price had gone down a few thousand, so, if nothing happened with the house…

For Sale by Auction

He saw the board and gave a smile as he read that the auction wasn't far off, just a few weeks away, in fact. And there was an 'open for inspection' scheduled at the weekend. Walking back toward the beach, this time he noticed the glorious skies and the stillness of the morning, seagulls sitting like ducks on the calm water, a dog running in and chasing them away. And then he saw *her*, standing in the glassy ocean, the water to her knees, legs apart and stretching, her hands reaching for the sky. She stood still and held the position and then slowly lowered her arms.

And then did it all over again.

God! Ben rolled his eyes. He had a great physique and made a very half-hearted attempt to keep it, relying mainly on walking a thousand miles a day in Emergency then burning it off with a swim, but this new-age, welcome-the-day-type stuff, or whatever she was doing…

Please!

Still, Ben conceded there *was* something rather spectacular about her lack of inhibition, something about her that made Ben smile as he walked.

And then she turned and his smile vanished as she bent over…doubled over, actually. Ben saw her swollen stomach and realised she was pregnant *and* visibly in pain. Picking up speed, he walked a touch more quickly along the sandy pathway and onto the beach—not wanting to overreact as maybe it was part of her exercise routine. But, no, she was walking uncomfortably out of the shallows now, still bent at an awkward angle, and Ben broke into a light jog, meeting her at the foreshore. He stared down at a mop of dark curls on the top of her head as, still bent over double, she held onto her knees.

'Are you okay?' he asked in concern.

'Fine,' she moaned, and then looked up. She had amber eyes and big silver earrings and was gritting her very white teeth. 'Stupid yoga!'

'Are you having a contraction?' He was assessing her. Not wanting to just dive in and place his hand on her stomach, he thought he ought to introduce himself first. 'I'm Ben, I'm a doctor…'

'And I'm Celeste.' She blew out a breath and then slowly unfolded. 'And I'm not having a contraction, it's a stitch.'

'You're sure?'

'Quite sure!' She stretched and winced and then rubbed the last of her stitch away. 'Stupid new-age stuff!' He couldn't help but smile and then so did she. 'According to my obstetrician, it's supposed to relax both me and the baby. It will kill us both, more like!'

He tensed, standing on the beach on a glorious warm morning, and was slammed back there again—just as he was almost every day, every night. Not all the time now but surely, given it was nearly four years on, *too* many times.

'So long as you're okay,' he clipped, and went to go, but she was holding her swollen stomach now with both hands and blowing out a long, slow breath. 'That,' Ben said firmly, 'is *not* a stitch.'

'No.' Her eyes screwed up just a touch and this time he did place his hand on her stomach, felt the weak tightening flowing around her uterus, and held his hand there till it passed, satisfied that it was nothing more than a Braxton-Hicks' contraction.

'It's just the baby practising for its big day.' She smiled. 'Honestly, I'm fine.'

'You're positive?' he pressed.

'Absolutely.'

'If they get stronger, or start coming—'

'More regularly, I know, I know.' She gave him a very wide smile. The sun was up now and he could see her tan and her freckly face. She really did have an incredible smile… 'Well, thanks anyway,' she said.

'No problem.'

She turned to walk along the beach, in the direction he was going, and as he started to walk behind her, he half watched her to make sure she didn't stop again, but she seemed fine now. Dressed in white shorts and a white tight-fitting top, she was curves everywhere, and Ben felt a touch awkward when her head turned around.

'I'm not following you—I live up there,' he explained.

'Good!' She slowed her pace down. 'Where?'

'In the units at the end.'

'Since when?' she asked.

'Since the weekend.'

'We're neighbours, then.' She smiled. 'I'm Celeste Mitchell, I live in Unit 3.'

'Ben, Ben Richardson—I'm at number 22."

'You're at the quiet end, then.' Celeste rolled her eyes.

'Are you sure about that?' Ben said, raising an eyebrow. 'It certainly hasn't been quiet the last two nights. Fights, parties…'

'That's nothing compared to *my* neighbours,' she retorted.

They were there now, at the row of one-bedroom units that were a bit of an eyesore in such lovely setting. No doubt one day a developer would come in and swoop up the lot of them and build a luxury complex or a hotel, but for now they were just an old and rather rundown row of units that offered cheap rental and beach access—and were filled with backpackers looking to settle for a few weeks and the occasional regular tenant, which Celeste obviously was.

As they walked past her unit, it stood out from the rest—the little strip of grass at the front had been mowed and there were pots of sunflowers in the small porch.

Clearly this was her home.

'Thanks again for your concern.' She grinned. 'And if you need a cup of sugar…'

He laughed. 'I'll know where to come.'

'I was going to say you'll have to go next door. The doctor just put me on a diet.'

He laughed again and waved goodbye. Heading up to his unit, he let himself in, put on the kettle and peered around the gloomy interior before heading for the cranky shower, wondering if it would spurt hot or cold this morning.

He hoped her flat was nicer than his. It was an odd thought to pop into his head, but he just hoped it was, that was all. It was certainly as neat as a pin on the outside—maybe her husband had painted it. And hopefully she had nicer furniture than his landlord had provided. Still, that wouldn't make up for the noise…

Coming out of the shower, he could hear his neighbours fighting again and for Ben the auction couldn't come soon enough.

He made some coffee and smiled again as he spooned in sugar.

She didn't need to be on diet—she was curvy, yes, but she was pregnant. He thought of that lovely round bottom, wiggling up the beach in front of him, and just the image of her, so crystal clear in his memory, startled him, so that he immediately turned his mind to more practical thoughts.

Her blood glucose was probably high. She'd be around seven months or so…

He forced himself to push her out of his head, and wouldn't let himself give her another thought—till he drove out of his garage, feeling just a touch uncomfortable in his slick four-wheel drive, and saw her watering her sunflowers and waving at him.

He waved back—reluctantly. Ben didn't like waving to neighbours or, despite what he had said, dropping in for sugar, or popping over for a chat. Had she not appeared in pain, he'd have kept right on walking, have kept himself to himself—which was just how he liked things to be.

Whoosh!

As he drove past, Celeste could feel her cheeks redden even as she, oh, so casually waved.

He. Was. Gorgeous!

Gorgeous! Well over six feet and broad, his legs were as thick and as solid as an international rugby player's, and that longish brown hair flopping over his eyes as he'd stared down at her on the beach already had her wanting to run her fingers through it. As for those green eyes…why the hell didn't they have doctors like that where she worked?

Then she stopped being twenty-four and single and remembered she had sworn off men for the next decade at least. Also, she was, in a few weeks, going to be a mum.

Funny, but for a moment she'd forgotten. Talking to Ben, chatting as they'd walked, for a moment there she'd forgotten she was pregnant, had just felt like, well, a normal woman! Which she was, of course—there was nothing more womanly or normal than pregnancy. But this morning she'd been one who'd fancied and blushed and said all the wrong things in the face of a very sexy man. Celeste had assumed, though she'd neither read nor been told it, that the 'fancy' switch remained off during pregnancy—that you went into some sort of hormonal seclusion, where men were no longer attractive and you didn't flirt or even look twice. And for six months it *had* been that way…

Would stay that way, Celeste told herself firmly.

Not that she needed to worry. A deft kick from her baby reminded her that she had no choice in the matter—she was hardly a candidate for romance!

CHAPTER TWO

'CELESTE, what are you doing here?' Meg, the charge nurse, shook her head as Celeste handed her a return-to-work certificate as she joined the late-shift emergency nurses to receive handover.

'I'm fine to work. I saw my obstetrician again yesterday,' Celeste explained.

Meg scanned the certificate and, sure enough, she had been declared fit, only Meg wasn't so sure. 'You were exhausted when I sent you home last week, Celeste. I was seriously worried about you.'

'I'm okay now—with my days off and a week's sick leave…' When Meg didn't look convinced Celeste relented and told her everything. 'My glucose tolerance test came in high, that's what the problem was, but I've been on a diet for ten days now, and I've been resting, doing yoga and taking walks on the beach. I feel fantastic—some people work right up to forty weeks!'

'Not in Emergency,' Meg said, 'and you're certainly not going to make it that far. How many weeks are you now?'

'Thirty,' Celeste said, 'and, as the doctor said, I'm fine.'

Which didn't give Meg any room to argue and,

anyway, here wasn't the place to try. Instead she took them through the whiteboard, giving some history on each of the patients in the cubicles and areas. 'When the observation ward opens, Celeste can go round there…'

'I don't need to be in Obs,' Celeste said, guilty that they were giving her the lightest shift, but Meg fixed her with a look.

'I don't have the resources to work around your pregnancy, Celeste. If your obstetrician says that you're fine for full duties and you concur, I have to go along with that—I'm just allocating the board.'

Celeste nodded, but no matter how forcibly Meg said it, Celeste knew she was being looked out for as far as her colleagues could—and for the ten zillionth time since she'd found out she was pregnant she felt guilty.

Finding out she was pregnant had been bad enough, but the fallout had been spectacular.

Her family was no longer speaking to her, especially as she had steadfastly refused to name the father, but how could she? Having found out that not only was her *boyfriend* married but that his wife worked in Admin at the hospital she worked in, even though no one knew, would ever know, guilt and shame had left Celeste with no choice but to hand in her notice. Then, just as it had all looked hopeless, she had found out that she been accepted at the graduate emergency nursing programme at Bay View Hospital, which was on the other side of the city.

She hadn't been pregnant at the time of her application and the polite thing to do might have been to defer—perhaps that was what had been expected of her—but with such an uncertain future ahead, a monthly pay cheque was essential in the short term, and, as a clearly single mother, more qualifications wouldn't go amiss. Also, moving away from home and friends would halt the endless questions.

It was lonely, though.

And now her colleagues were having to make concessions—no matter how much they denied that they were.

'Cubicle seven is Matthew Dale, eighteen years old. A minor head injury, he tripped while jogging, no LOC. He should be discharged, Ben's seeing him now.'

'Ben?' Celeste checked.

'The new registrar. He started this morning. Here he is now…' Meg waved him over. 'What's happening with cubicle seven, Ben?'

'I'm going to keep him in. Sorry to open up the observation ward so early but…' His voice trailed off as he caught sight of Celeste, but for whatever reason he chose not to acknowledge her, just carried on giving his orders for the patient. Although she had to offer him *no* explanation as to her being here, and though there was absolutely no reason to, again, for the ten zillionth and first time, Celeste felt guilty.

Almost as if she'd been caught.

Doing what? Celeste scolded herself, as she walked round to the closed-off observation ward, flicked on the lights and then turned back a bed for Matthew.

She was earning a living—she *had* to earn a living.

She had ten weeks of pregnancy to go and the crèche wouldn't take the baby till it had had all its inoculations, so if she stopped now she wouldn't be working for almost six months.

The panic that was permanently just a moment away washed over her.

How was she going to cope?

Even working full time it was a struggle to meet the rent. With no help from her family, she was saving for the stroller and cot and had bought some teeny, tiny baby clothes and some nappies, but there was so much more she needed. Then there was her bomb of a car...

Celeste could actually *feel* her panic rising as she faced the impossibility of it all and she willed herself to be calm, willed herself to slow her racing mind down. But that was no help either, because the second she stopped panicking all Celeste felt was exhausted.

Holding the bed sheet in her hand, she actually wanted to climb in, to lie down and pull the sheet over her head and sleep—and get fatter—and read baby magazines and feel kicks and just *rest*.

'Feeling better?' Celeste jumped at the sound of Ben's voice. 'After this morning?'

'I had a stitch,' Celeste responded just a touch too sharply. 'And, before you ask, I am quite capable of working. I'm sick of people implying that I shouldn't be here. Pregnancy isn't a disease, you know!'

'I was just being polite.' Ben gave her a slightly wide-eyed look. 'Making conversation—you know, with my neighbour?'

She'd overreacted, she knew that, and an apology was in order. 'I'm sorry—I've had a bit of trouble convincing the doctor that I'm capable of coming back to work, and I've got Meg questioning me here. I just...'

'Don't need it.'

'Exactly,' Celeste said. 'I'm hardly going to put the baby at risk.'

'Good.'

She waited for the 'but,' for him to elaborate, for the little short, sharp lecture that she seemed to be getting a lot these days, but 'good' was all he said. Well, it was all he said about her condition, anyway.

'I've booked Matthew in for a scan. He had a small vomit, and I'd rather play safe. He's a bit pale, and I'm just not happy—they should call round for him soon. I've also found a hand injury to keep you occupied…' He gave her a nice smile and handed her the notes. 'Fleur Edwards, eighty-two years of age. She's got a nasty hand laceration, probable tendon, though the surgeons won't be able to fit her in till much later tonight. Given her age, it will be under local anaes-thetic, so if you can give her a light lunch and then fast her—elevation IV antis, the usual.'

'Sure.'

'Could you run a quick ECG on her, too? No rush.'

He was nice and laid-back, Celeste thought. He didn't talk down to her just because she was a grad, didn't ream off endless instructions as if she'd never looked after a head injury or hand laceration before. And, best of all, he hadn't lectured her on whether she should be here.

The observation ward was rather like a bus-stop—you were either standing or sitting around waiting, with nothing much happening for ages or everything arriving at once.

Matthew was brought around first, pale, as Ben had

described, but he managed a laugh as he climbed up onto the bed as Celeste had a joke with him.

'You do know exercise is bad for you?' His mother and girlfriend had both come around to see him into the observation ward, but now he was there and settled they would be heading home. Celeste did a careful set of neurological observations, warning Matthew this would be happening on the hour, every hour. 'Whether you're asleep or not…'

She told Matthew's family about visiting and discharge times and wrote down the hospital and extension numbers for them. Just as she was about to get started on the admission paperwork, the doors opened.

'Another admission for you…' Deb, a fellow grad, was wheeling round a rather delightful Fleur—with rouged cheeks and painted on eyebrows, she was dressed in a blue and white polka-dot skirt with a smart white blouse, which unfortunately had been splattered with blood. 'Fleur Edwards, 82, a hand injury—' Deb started.

'Ben's already told me about her,' Celeste said, sensing Deb was in a rush. 'Any family?'

'Her daughter's coming in this afternoon.' They flicked through the charts. 'No allergies, she suffers with arthritis, but apart from that she seems very well…'

'I'll sort things out, then,' Celeste said, smiling over at Fleur, who was patiently sitting in a wheelchair, her arm in a sling. 'Is it getting busy out there?' she asked Deb.

'It's starting to—we've got a multi-trauma coming in.'

Though she smiled as she went over to help Fleur, Celeste was hit with a pang as Deb left, just a pang of *something.* She should be out there, would have loved to really immerse herself in this emergency programme, and though she hoped to when she came back from maternity leave, Celeste was also realistic enough to know that her head would be full of other things by then, and that she'd be exhausted for other reasons, namely the baby who was kicking at her diaphragm right now. Still, it wasn't Fleur's problem.

'Hello, Mrs Edwards.'

'Fleur.' Fleur smiled.

'I'm Celeste—I'll be looking after you this shift.'

'You should be the one being looked after.' Fleur clucked. She really was gorgeous. Widowed for twenty years, she was an independent old lady, and she had cut her hand peeling an orange for her morning snack, Celeste found out as she took her history.

'Well, for now we'll get you into a gown and into bed, so that we can elevate your hand on an IV pole. You've had something for pain—has that helped?'

'I can hardly feel it, the bandage is so tight.' Fleur said. 'Would you mind taking me over to the ladies' before I get into bed?'

'Of course.' Only at that moment Matthew sat up, with that anxious, frantic look Celeste knew all too well, and with a quick 'Won't be a moment' to Fleur she raced over, locating a kidney dish just in time and pulling the curtain around him.

'It's okay, Matthew,' she soothed. 'I'll just fetch you a wet cloth…' And run another set of obs, Celeste thought. He really was terribly pale.

'I've got to get work,' Matthew muttered. He wasn't

a particularly large 18-year-old, but none the less he was trying to climb out of bed and he resisted as Celeste tried to guide him to lie back down. 'I have to get to work, I'm going to be late…'

'You're in hospital, Matthew,' Celeste said. 'You've had a bang on your head, remember?'

She was trying to reach for the call bell to summon help, worried that if he became agitated he might fall if he did get out of bed and hurt himself further, but as quickly as it had happened, Matthew seemed to remember where he was and stopped trying to climb out of bed and instead lay back down. 'Sorry.' He gave a wan smile and said it again. 'Sorry. I'm fine now.' And he seemed so, except, like Ben, Celeste was now worried.

'Matthew. Do you know where you are?'

'Hospital.'

She went through his obs—they were the same as before, his blood pressure a smudge higher, but his momentary confusion still troubled Celeste and she buzzed on the intercom. 'Can you send a doctor round to the observation ward?'

'Is it urgent?' Meg checked. 'They're just assessing a multi-trauma.' Celeste looked over at Matthew's pale but relaxed face and wavered for a moment. He seemed absolutely fine now and his obs were stable but, still, she just wasn't sure.

'I need the head injury assessed again,' she said, thinking it was likely Meg was rolling her eyes now. 'Let Ben know—he saw him.' She headed back to Matthew and Fleur gave a worried nod when Celeste said, 'I'll be with you soon.'

'Look after him!' the old lady said. 'Don't worry about me.'

Of course, by the time Ben arrived Matthew was sitting up and joking about his moment of confusion and refusing the oxygen that Celeste was trying to give him. 'Look, I'm sorry to pull you away,' she told Ben.

'No problem. The trauma team is with the patient and he's actually not that bad. So what's going on with Matthew?'

'Nothing!' Matthew said and it certainly looked that way.

'He was fine,' Celeste explained. 'In fact, he seems fine now, but he had a vomit a little earlier and was certainly confused and restless for a moment. He didn't look at all well—' She was trying to think up reasons to justify pulling a registrar out from an emergency, but Ben quickly interrupted.

'I agree.'

He didn't seem remotely annoyed that she had called him. Instead, he was checking Matthew's pupils and his blood pressure for himself as Celeste explained that he had tried to climb out of bed, insisting he had to get to work.

'How are you feeling, Matthew?'

'Fine. Well, a bit of a headache...'

'Okay,' Ben said, 'I'm just going to lay you flat and have a good look at you.' It was Ben who never got to finish this time as Matthew started to retch again, his face more grey than pale now, and he was moaning loudly about a pain in his head.

'How do you get urgent help around here?' Ben

asked, and it was only then that Celeste remembered that it was his first day here—he seemed so assured and competent. He was also a lot bigger than Matthew. He ignored the patient's protests to push off the oxygen mask and attempts to climb out of bed as Celeste pressed the switch on the wall. The light flashed above the door like a strobe as one of the team came to the intercom and Celeste explained what was happening.

The trauma team was still with the multi-trauma, so it was Belinda Hamilton, the rather snooty but exceptionally good-looking senior emergency registrar who came, along with Meg and a porter to get the patient to Resus if required. Had Matthew still been on a gurney it would have been easier to wheel him straight to Resus, but time was of the essence and the observation ward was set up, like any other ward, for such an emergency, so instead Celeste wheeled over the crash trolley. Matthew was like a tethered bull now, and it was Ben doing the tethering as he rapidly explained what had occurred to his senior. But he didn't await her verdict, just told her what was required. 'He needs to intubated and sent for a scan,' Ben said. 'Can you alert the neuro surgeons?'

Celeste was busy opening packs for the intubation, her heart hammering in her chest, stunned at how quickly Matthew had deteriorated.

Though Meg had also come to assist, she didn't take over, just guided and advised Celeste, who was setting up for the intubation. Raji, the anaesthetist, arrived just as Matthew started seizing, his body jerking violently. The whole thing was horrible. In a matter of moments

Matthew's condition had become critical—his family would have barely made it to the car park.

Raji was shooting drugs into the patient as Ben gave him the lowdown and thankfully the jerking stopped. Matthew was taking long, laboured breaths, but at least he wasn't seizing or fighting any more, though Celeste could feel her blood pounding, surely up near Matthew's as she wrestled to remove the bedhead to give Raji more access to the patient's airway.

'Here.' Ben must have seen her struggle and removed the bedhead easily for her. Raji was a pleasure to work with, a laid-back guy who really just got on with things, checking all the drugs she had prepared and pulling up for himself the others he required. Matthew was on a cardiac monitor, the seizing had stopped, but he was gravely ill and as Celeste watched Raji intubate the patient, Meg liaised with the porters and Imaging.

'Should we let his family know?' Celeste asked. 'They only just left.'

'Let's just worry about the patient for now,' Belinda snapped, and Celeste felt herself redden.

'I'll call them as soon as I can,' Ben said. 'He'll probably go straight up to Theatre from Imaging.'

It took ten, maybe fifteen minutes at the most before Matthew was paralysed and intubated and on a trolley, being wheeled up to Imaging and probably then on to Theatre. All that was left from his time in the obs ward was a mountain of paperwork and a lot of chaos. The suction equipment was still on and gurgling, and would need cleaning, the oxygen tubing and masks would need replacing; the bedhead was abandoned on the other side of the room, there were packs open everywhere. The crash cart was in chaos and there were syringes and vials on its surface. Everything would need to be tidied and checked and replaced and then checked again.

'So much for giving you a quiet afternoon!' Meg gave her a sympathetic smile, but her pager went off, and there really was no chance of her staying to help.

Letting out a long breath, forcing herself to just get on with it, Celeste turned around and saw Fleur's worried face.

'Will he be okay?' she asked worriedly.

'I think so,' Celeste said, and came over, her heart sinking as the proud, dignified lady burst into tears and said sorry over and over.

'I've wet my pants!'

'I'm so sorry!' It was Celeste saying it to Fleur now. 'It was my fault for not taking you.'

Ben was at the desk ringing the unfortunate family to tell them what had happened to Matthew, and Celeste and Fleur were in the bathroom. Fleur's wet clothes were off and her hand was wrapped in plastic and elevated on an IV pole, with the old lady sitting in a little shower chair.

'Let's both stop saying sorry, shall we?' A lot older and a lot wiser, Fleur caught Celeste's eyes and smiled. 'You could hardly leave the young man, could you?'

'I know.'

'I just don't want my daughter to know that I've had an accident—she'll be in soon, and she'll think I'm losing my faculties.'

'Of course you're not!' Celeste exclaimed. Still, she'd have been embarrassed too, so she came up with a plan. 'Why don't I rinse out your clothes?' Celeste suggested. 'They're covered in blood anyway. I'll tell your daughter that's why I washed them.'

'What about my knickers?'

'I'll wash them and hang them by the vent.' A little bit ditzy at times, Celeste could also be very practical. 'They'll be dry by the end of my shift—no one will ever know.'

'You're very kind.'

Not really, Celeste thought. Anyone should do it. She still winced when nurses stuffed filthy clothes into bags for relatives, wondering how they'd like it. Still, she couldn't change the world, only her own actions. So she filled a sink with water…

'Cold water for blood,' Fleur prompted, and Celeste did as she was told then set about showering her patient. Firm friends now, Celeste smiled when Fleur asked what was surely a rare favour. 'Would you mind giving my back an good wash?' she asked. 'I can never reach it.'

'Of course.' Fleur's back was indeed grubby from, most likely, years of neglect, as her arthritis simply wouldn't allow her arms to reach it.

'I bought a brush from the chemist,' Fleur said as Celeste gave it a good scrub. 'You know, on a long stick, but I still can't get there.' So Celeste took her time to wash it as thoroughly as she could, wondering how best to approach this proud lady.

'You'll be needing some help with your hand out of action…'

'I will not!' Fleur said, as Celeste wrapped her in towels. 'I'll manage fine with one hand.'

'You probably will,' Celeste said, 'but there are so many aids, like hand-held showers, and there are brushes for your back but with curved sticks. I'm not sure of all the things that could help, but maybe we could get you assessed.'

'I like my independence.'

'Well, this will help you keep your independence.' Celeste shrugged. 'You may as well while you're here… Have a think about it.'

Fleur was right, Ben thought. Sitting at the desk for a moment, having made a very difficult call to Matthew's mother and not ready to head back out there, he'd overheard the conversation between the two women. Celeste *was* kind, very kind indeed.

It was so easy to become hard working in Emergency— he'd seen it happen to so many colleagues. It was necessary almost if you wanted to survive in this area. He had become hardened too—switched off on certain occasions, because at times it was easier to deal with a patient than a person, kinder to yourself not to think about a family and friends and futures that were being obliterated, to just get on with the job in hand, rather than look at the bigger picture. But watching Celeste wheel out a smiling Fleur, all powdered and warm and well looked after, Ben was a mite conflicted.

Because pregnancy was his *thing*. One of his many *things* if he actually stopped and thought about it, which he tried very hard not to do.

Most people had one—Belinda had just told him on

the walk back from Imaging how her younger brother had almost died from a head injury. The staff hadn't noticed his deterioration and it had been Belinda herself who had recognised the signs when she had come to visit. Yes, they all had their *things*. And pregnancy was Ben's—the one thing where he just had to detach and deal with a foetus rather than a baby, look at a set of numbers instead of the person.

He didn't want to be hard, didn't want to be bitter—except he was.

Yet watching Celeste rub her back after helping Fleur into bed, reluctantly watching the shape of her pregnant belly, he resisted the urge to just walk away, to shrug his shoulders and let her get on with it. She wasn't a nurse, or a set of numbers, or a pregnant woman, she was Celeste, who was kind and tired and had had a difficult start to her shift and a lot of mess to clean up.

'I've spoken to Matthew's family…' As he chatted to her, he lifted the metal bedhead from the floor and replaced it, then easily dragged the portable oxygen cylinder back to its spot—just doing a couple of little things that he didn't need to, in the same way Celeste had done for Fleur, only she could never know the effort behind his easy gestures, because being around her was becoming unbearable for Ben. 'They're on their way back. I've told them to come to the front desk, but if they arrive here, just give me a buzz.'

'I will.' She pulled over a linen skip and stripped the bed. 'Do you think he'll be okay?'

'He'll be in Theatre by now,' Ben said, 'so, hopefully, yes. I'll let you know when I hear.'

Her quiet shift was anything but. By the time it came to a close the crash cart was checked and put away, the eight beds had been filled with patients, Fleur had agreed to a visit from Occupational Therapy and now that visiting time was over, the ward was actually neat and in order—at least the night nurse should have a quiet shift!

'Thank you, Celeste.' Fleur smiled as Celeste helped her into clean, dry undies before she headed off home. 'For all your care and for washing out my clothes—my daughter never suspected a thing.'

'That's good. Theatre just called and it shouldn't be too much longer till they're ready for you.'

'And I'll just stay in for one night?'

'If all goes smoothly, which I'm sure it will. I'll see you in the morning.' Celeste smiled. 'I'm back on at seven.'

'You work too hard,' Fleur fussed. 'I know it's what you girls do now. Still, I hope your young man's at home with dinner waiting so you can put your feet up.'

'I shall!' Celeste smiled and then blushed as she realised that Ben had come in. ''Night, Fleur.' She walked over to Ben. 'I don't want her worrying.'

'Sorry?'

Celeste hurried to explain. 'Well, it's just easier to sometimes let people think that there is a Mr Mitchell at home…' Her blush darkened as it was only then she realised Ben would have neither known nor cared that she had just been caught fibbing to Fleur. 'Have you heard anything about Matthew?'

'That's what I was coming to tell you about. I'm heading home, so I just rang ICU. I didn't get a chance till now. Apparently his pupil blew in Imaging. They got him straight up to theatre and evacuated a massive subdural haematoma—so I came to say well done. It was a good pick-up—a lot of people might have hesitated seeing as his symptoms were so fleeting.'

'How is he now?' Celeste asked, warming at his praise. Matthew's brain had been bleeding, the pressure building inside his skull, causing his symptoms. It was the scary thing about seemingly benign head injuries—and the reason patients were often admitted for observation afterwards. She had read about it, studied it, learnt about it, but now she had witnessed it for herself. The *chore* of regular neuro obs would never be considered a chore again.

'On ICU. It will be a good forty-eight hours before we know anything, but there is hope…'

Which was always nice.

She handed over her patients and headed for home in a car that was making more new and rather worrying noises. She slowed down at the gates and indicated left for the block of units. She climbed out of the car, leaving it idling, too worried to turn off the engine, because one day it surely wouldn't start again! Absolutely bone weary, she opened the gates and then realised someone had pulled up behind her.

'I'll close them,' Ben called out, which he did, and she drove another hundred yards and then pulled on her handbrake and climbed out of her idling car again to open the garage, because the landlord was too mean to put in automatic doors.

'I'll get that.' He walked over from the gates and made light work of the garage door, and even waited till she had driven inside and closed it for her as she walked out.

Which didn't sound like much, but every stretch was one less stretch that she had to do and she was so tired that all she was was grateful.

'Thanks for that.' Celeste was too weary to even summon a smile.

'No problem,' Ben called, heading back to his own car to repeat the ritual for his own garage. And still he didn't deliver a lecture. Still didn't check that she was okay, or ask if she was sure she should be working.

Had he asked, Celeste thought, as she let herself into her little unit, she might just have burst into tears.

She had to eat, but she was too tired to cook, so she had a bowl of cereal instead.

Then a very quick shower. Knowing she'd regret it if she didn't, she put out a fresh uniform for the morning, checked her alarm and slipped into bed, too tired to worry, too worn out for tears or even to think really.

She had to be back there tomorrow at ten to seven!

CHAPTER THREE

BEN didn't worry.

He was concerned for his patients at times, but he didn't do worrying.

The worst day of his life had happened a long time ago and he knew things could never be that bad again, so consequently he just got on with things, didn't fret or dwell—or, well, worry!

He hadn't in years.

Yet there was this niggle now and, no matter how he tried to ignore it, still it persisted.

His second day at Bay View Hospital and the flood-gates had opened.

One drowning had been brought in as well as victims of a multiple pile-up on the beach road. It was over forty degrees and people were collapsing everywhere. It was just one of those days where everyone ran to keep up and everyone worked up to and beyond their limits.

Including Celeste.

He could see her ankles swelling as the shift progressed, see her blow out of her mouth and onto her red face as she stripped yet another trolley and prepared it for the endless list of recipients, could see the *effort* in her movements, and then finally the sheer relief on her face at 3:30 p.m. when her shift ended. As he watched her waddle out, like it or not, Ben *was* worried.

'What are you doing tonight?' Belinda was tapping away on the computer. In her late thirties, and absolutely stunning, she was also witty. With a tumble of black hair, she had almond-shaped brown eyes, full red lips, and dressed like she'd stepped out of a magazine. Thankfully, *very* thankfully, Ben didn't fancy her a jot, which meant there was no trouble sharing a tiny office and they could chat easily about things—which they did as Ben wound up his day and packed up his briefcase. It was only his second day and already paperwork was starting to pile up.

'I'm stopping in at the real-estate agent's, then the deli to buy salad and chicken instead of a burger and then…' Ben thought about it '…I will *make* myself go for a jog this evening. What about you?'

'I'll show you…' She gave a wicked smile. 'Come here.'

Curious, Ben walked over and looked at the screen and stared at the image of a rather ordinary-looking guy.

'A GP, late thirties, has children but doesn't want to involve them yet…'

'Sorry?' Ben had no idea what she was going on about.

'That's good,' Belinda said. 'The last one I saw brought his children along on the second date! We've chatted on the phone,' Belinda explained to a bemused Ben, 'and he seems great—we're meeting for coffee tonight.'

'You're going on a *date* with him?'

'Coffee.' Belinda laughed. 'You should try it—you'd be a hit!'

Ben shook his head. 'Internet dating isn't for me.'

'Don't knock it till you try it.'

'Be careful.' Ben frowned. 'Shouldn't you go with someone when you meet him? He could be anyone!'

'He's who he says is.' Belinda winked. 'I've checked his registration.'

'Well, good luck.'

The real-estate agent was being nice to him again—there had been a little bit of initial sulking when Ben hadn't bought the apartment, but he'd obviously got over it and he was Ben's new best friend again now that he had a genuine prospective client for the house.

'Can I have a look around?' Ben asked.

'Not till the "open for inspection" at the weekend,' the agent said. 'After that, I can arrange a private inspection for you.'

'I'm actually working this weekend,' Ben said, 'so don't worry about it.'

'You will come and have a look, though?' the agent said anxiously.

'Like I said…' Ben shrugged '…I'm working—but it's really no problem. I'm actually going to look at another house tonight.'

That soon got him on the phone! A private inspection was arranged within the hour and Ben wandered through the house he was seriously thinking of calling home. It did need a lot of work—the kitchen was a bomb and the downstairs bathroom would need to be ripped out, but the master bedroom had already been renovated, with floor-to-ceiling windows that took in the bay view and a fantastic en suite that did the same.

Yes, it was way too big for one, but it just felt right.

He could renovate it, Ben thought, take his time, pull out the kitchen, do up the back garden… Standing in the master bedroom, staring out at the bay, Ben felt the first breeze of contentment he had in years, the first, the very first glimmer of how finally coming home should feel.

Despite his nonchalance with the agent, despite the shake of his head when he found out the reserve price and that the vendor wanted a quick settlement, he was just playing the necessary game. For Ben, the auction couldn't come soon enough.

A wall of heat hit him as Ben opened the door to his unit. He opened the windows, turned on a fan and put his dinner in the fridge then peeled off his clothes and hoped that the shower ran cold this evening—which thankfully it did.

After showering, he pulled on some shorts and nothing else, then headed for the kitchen. Suddenly, out of the blue, there was this sort of long groan as everything ground to a halt.

It had been happening all over Melbourne—the power outages every evening as the lucky people who had air-conditioning selfishly cranked it up to full. Ben just had a fan—which now, of course, wasn't working.

He went outside to check the power box, just in case it was only him, and glancing down the row of units he saw Celeste checking her power box too.

She was in lilac shorts this time, and a black singlet. Her hair was wet and she looked thoroughly fed up.

'Again!' She rolled her eyes, gave him a brief wave and headed back into what would surely soon be a furnace—unlike his unit, Celeste's got the full questionable glory of the afternoon sun.

And that was when that niggle hit him again—an unfamiliar, long-forgotten feeling that gnawed at his stomach as he pulled open the dark fridge and pulled out the plastic containers he had got from the deli—a strange niggle of worry for someone else.

Ben didn't want neighbours who dropped in on him and he had certainly never thought he'd be a neighbour who did just that—but there he was on her doorstep. She had come to the door holding a bowl of cereal and was clearly irritated at the intrusion but trying to be polite.

'The electricity should come back on in a couple of hours—it's been happening a lot lately,' Celeste said, and went to close the door. She wasn't actually irritated with him and didn't mean to be rude, she was just trying not to notice he was wearing only shorts. Which was normal, of course, in the middle of a heat wave. Had he knocked just two minutes later, she'd have had to put her top back on herself before answering the door!

The sight of all his exposed skin made her own turn pink, though, and she didn't want him to notice!

'Have you had dinner?' he said to the closing door, and she paused, glancing guiltily down at the bowl of cereal—which was probably not the best dinner for a heavily pregnant woman and she was instantly on the defensive. 'I can hardly cook with no electricity.'

'No need to—I've got plenty.' He held up the dishes to tempt her. 'Let's go and eat on the beach—it will be cooler there.'

It was. There was a lovely southerly breeze sweeping in and Celeste walked in the shallows. Ben could practically hear the sizzle as her hot, swollen, red ankles hit the water.

'I should have come down earlier.' Celeste sighed in relief. 'I keep meaning to, I mean, I'm so glad I did when I get here…'

'I'm the same.' Ben smiled, and it was so nice after such a busy day to just walk and say not much, to watch the dogs and the boats and the couples—to just *be*.

And then to sit.

Chicken in tarragon and mayonnaise, with a crisp Greek salad, was certainly nicer than cereal, and washed down with fresh fruit salad, it was bordering on the healthiest dinner of her pregnancy. The baby gave an appreciative kick as she sank down onto her back.

'That was yum—thank you!'

'You're welcome.' Ben gave a small uncomfortable swallow. 'Look, I'm sorry if I dismissed you a bit at work.'

'You didn't.' Celeste frowned.

'I did,' Ben said, 'or rather I didn't let on that we'd already met.'

'That's okay.'

'I just like to keep work separate…'

'That's fine,' Celeste said. 'This evening never happened.' She turned and smiled at him where he still sat. 'How are you enjoying your new job?'

'It's good.' Ben nodded.

'You were in Sydney before?' Celeste checked because she'd heard Meg say so.

'Yes.' Ben didn't elaborate. 'How long have you worked there?'

She didn't reply for a moment as she was busy settling herself back on the sand, closing her eyes in sheer pleasure. 'Nearly three months.' One eye peeked open. 'I don't think they were particularly thrilled when I turned up for my first shift.'

Thankfully he wasn't so politically correct that he pretended to have no idea what she was talking about. Instead, he just grinned and Celeste closed that eye and finally, finally, finally she relaxed.

'God, this feels nice,' she sighed after five minutes of lovely comfortable silence.

And it also looked nice, Ben thought, it looked very nice indeed. Her lashes were fanning her cheeks, her knees were up, and her stomach was sort of wriggling of its own accord—like Jennifer's had, Ben thought, and then abruptly stopped that thought process.

'So there is no Mr Mitchell?' he asked.

'Nope.' Her eyes were still closed.

'Do you see him at all, the father of your baby?'

'Nope.'

'Does he know?' Ben asked, even though it was none of his business. 'I mean, is he helping you out?'

'He thought he was,' Celeste said. 'He gave me money to have an abortion.'

'Oh.' Ben stared down at her.

'I was on my maternity rotation at the time I found

out I was pregnant, babies everywhere—not that it made me want one, it terrified me actually, but…'

'You don't have to say anything else if you don't want to.'

But she did want to—lying there with her eyes closed, lost and lonely and really, really confused. Maybe, as everyone said it would, talking might help clear her head. It was worth a try, anyway, because yoga certainly hadn't worked!

'He's married.' She opened her eyes then and closed them—and even in that teeny space of time she saw *it* pass over his features. That moment where you were judged, where opinions were cast, where assumptions were made. 'I didn't know that he was, not that that changes anything.'

'Did you go out for long?' he wanted to know.

'Three months.' Celeste sniffed. 'He was my first real… I just believed him. I mean, I knew why we didn't go out much, and why we couldn't go to each other's homes…'

'Sorry?'

'It doesn't matter,' she muttered.

'So where did you go out?'

'For drives, for dinner, to a hotel sometimes…' She gazed up into his clear green eyes. 'He's a bit older than me, quite a bit older actually,' Celeste said, and then she was silent for a while.

Rightly or wrongly, he did judge—he tried not to, but he did.

Why didn't people think? Why were people so careless?

And now there was this baby…

He closed his eyes and thought of Jennifer—of the plans they had put in place, how much they had wanted a baby, and though he didn't say a word, she could feel his disapproval.

'So you've never made a mistake?' she said defensively.

'I've made plenty,' he admitted.

'But no affairs, nothing you regret.'

'Oh, there's a lot that I regret,' Ben said.

'You're single, divorced…?' It sounded like the questionnaire on Belinda's dating site, and he winced inwardly.

'Widowed,' he said, and it was her turn to judge, Ben knew—he had been through it many times before.

'Do you miss her a lot?' she asked gently.

'Yep,' Ben admitted, and that was enough. He ran some sand through his hands, concentrated on the little grains instead of himself then glanced at his watch. 'The power must be back on by now.'

'So what if it is?' Celeste smiled. 'I'm enjoying talking—you were saying how much you miss her?'

God, she was persistent. Really, he should stand up and leave, but she'd said so much about herself and, picking up another handful of sand, he let it run through his closed fist, and admitted some of his truth. 'I miss it for Jennifer too.' Her silence was patient. 'She loved living.' He looked out to the water and could almost see her, blonde ponytail flying as she jogged. 'She'd be out there running or swimming now—cramming some exercise in after work.'

'Was she fit?'

'Very.' Ben nodded, but there was this savage rip of

thought there because, despite doing everything right, despite her healthy lifestyle, it hadn't counted for anything in the end.

'What did she do?'

'She was a doctor as well—in Emergency.'

'What happened?' Celeste asked, but Ben shook his head, not willing to go there. 'Come on.' It really was time to go now, and not just because he didn't want to talk about it. He was doing her a favour. A woman in Celeste's condition really didn't need to hear about how Jen had died. So he held her hands and heaved her up and they walked back slowly, idly chatting about not very much at all, till Celeste wormed her way back in again.

'Have you dated again—I mean since…?'

'She died three, nearly four years ago,' Ben said, answering the unspoken question.

'Oh.'

'A bit.' He gave a shrug. 'Though it was probably too soon.'

'Are you still comparing them to her?' Celeste asked, boldly striding in where no one else really dared to go, but Ben just ignored her question and, glad of the diversion, opened the gates to the units, but Celeste stood patiently waiting.

'Are you?' she asked.

'Sorry?'

'Comparing them?'

She was a persistent little thing, like a little woodpecker, peck, peck pecking away—

'I used to,' Ben admitted. 'But not now—that's not fair on anyone.'

'Especially as she sounds like Superwoman,' Celeste grumbled, and her response was so refreshing Ben actually smiled. 'So,' she pushed, 'are you ready now?'

'Perhaps, though not anything serious.'

'Ooh, I'm sure there'll be plenty of takers.' Celeste grinned. After all, she'd heard the giggles and gossip in the staffroom—Ben could take his pick!

'What about you?' They were sitting on her steps now, the conversation, and the friendship, too new, too fragile to snap it by asking him in. And anyway the power was still off, so they sat on the steps and got to know each other just a little bit better.

'I'm hardly in a position to date.' Celeste rolled her eyes. 'Can you imagine me out clubbing?'

'I guess not!'

'And I'm still in that "all men are snakes" place.'

'It's probably a very wise place to be right now,' Ben agreed. 'I've been a bit of a snake myself lately.'

'Do tell!' She did make him laugh, she was so eager for gossip, and so easy to talk to, that somehow he did.

'I went out with someone for a while—she was great, but even though I told her from the start—'

'She didn't listen?' she finished for him.

'She did at first, said she wanted the same thing—then, well, it got a bit more serious. She started to hint at wanting different things.' He looked into her smiling amber eyes. 'Like moving in.'

'Not for you?' she said wisely.

'Maybe one day, but she also started talking about children. And one thing I do know is that I don't want kids.'

'Never?'

'Never,' he said emphatically.

She got the message and was actually rather grateful for it. Oh, they hardly knew each other, had barely scratched the surface, but there was certainly if not an immediate attraction then at the very least an acute awareness. Which was something she hadn't felt in the longest time—had been sure, after the way Dean had treated her, that she'd never feel it again. But sitting here, looking into Ben's green eyes, hearing his words, Celeste suddenly realised that he felt it too. That he was carefully reading out the rules of any potential relationship should they choose to pursue one.

'We couldn't be less suited really,' Celeste said after a moment's pause. 'I'm not looking at all, you're not looking for serious and…' she patted her large stomach '…this isn't a hernia!'

'I had worked that out!' Ben smiled. 'So how about we just be friends?'

She stared into his green eyes and this time she didn't blush. Oh, she had a teeny crush on him—what heterosexual woman wouldn't?—but her heart was way too bruised and her ego far too raw and her soul just too tender to even fathom going there again. It was simply nice to have an adult to talk to. Her world had changed so much, and with her family not talking to her and her struggle to fit in on her new course, it was just nice, very nice to have Ben in her life, to talk to a person instead of staring at the television. 'A friend would be lovely.'

And still he stayed. Celeste went in and brought out two glasses of water, and then picked at daisies as they chatted, shredding them with her fingers, joining them up, and when she wasn't looking at him, somehow it made it easier for Ben to talk.

'You see, I had it all with Jen…' He pushed his fingers through his hair, tried to sum up how he was feeling, because she was so easy to talk to. Maybe because she hadn't known Jen, maybe because her eyes didn't well up with tears as friends' and family's did when he spoke about her, or flinch in tiny reproach at his sometimes bungling efforts to try and move on with his life. 'I don't want to try to re-create it—I don't want to do it again with someone else. I've already been there and done it.'

'Lucky you, then.' Ben blinked at her response. Really, he felt anything but lucky, but he supposed that, yes, she was right, he had been lucky to have Jen in his life for a while.

'I'd give anything to be able to say to this little one that its dad and I were in love.'

'Were you?' Ben asked.

'I thought so.' She shrugged. 'But looking back it was just infatuation, I guess—it sounds like you had the real thing.'

He didn't answer, because at that moment her television started blaring through the window, a cheer coming from the unit opposite as the power kicked back in.

'I'm going to do some work…' Ben stood up.

'Well, thank you for dinner…' Celeste smiled '…and a thank-you from the baby too.'

'You're very welcome.'

'I'd offer to return the favour, only I'm having enough trouble rustling up dinner for one at the moment,' she said wryly.

'I don't expect you to.'

He didn't expect her to. Celeste knew that and so too did Ben.

But next night when he came home from work he could see pots of sunflowers on his doorstep, her way of saying thank you, he guessed.

'I have some good news for you,' Ben said as he knocked on her door.

'I could do with some. Come in,' she invited.

'Matthew was extubated this evening,' Ben explained as he followed her into her tiny kitchen. 'He's doing really well—they're hoping to move him from ICU in the morning.'

That *was* good news!

'It could have been a very different story. I've had Belinda patting me on the back and the neuro consultant even came down to Emergency to say well done. I have told them that the credit goes to you.' He watched her face pink up with his praise. 'I know it's tough deciding whether to wait and see or call for help.'

'It can be,' Celeste admitted, as she pulled a vast jug of iced tea from the fridge and poured them both a long glass. 'I mean, you don't want to look like an idiot or that you're overreacting to everything…'

'Overreact!' Ben said simply. 'For now at least—until you've got more experience and your hunch button's working properly.'

'Hunch button?' Celeste frowned at the unfamiliar term. 'What's that?'

'When you have a hunch about something, when you're almost sure but not quite.'

She'd already worked out what he meant even before he explained it, but as he did explain it, she felt that glow in her cheeks darken just a touch, aware that he wasn't quite meeting her eyes. Her hunch button was tapping away, but for different reasons now, and she flicked it off quickly.

She was so not going to develop a crush on *another* man from work!

Look where that had got her!

And it *was* nice to have a friend.

They sat in her little living room, watching the 'weigh-in' on her favourite show, Celeste grumbling that she should be a contestant. Ben was more than a touch uncomfortable and trying not to show it—he could see the little pile of baby clothes all neatly folded on the ironing board and even though it was weeks away, there was a slight baby smell to the house—which probably had something to do with the baby lotion Celeste was rubbing into her hands, but still… So he went to get the jug of iced tea and when he came back, he poured her one into the glass she was holding, and he wouldn't have been human if he hadn't noticed her cleavage—would have to be blind to miss it actually, only Ben wasn't usually a breast man. Except that they were so jiggly and voluptuous that he was suddenly kneed in the groin with an unfamiliar longing.

So he sat down. He realised he couldn't smell that baby smell any more, just the unsettling scent of Celeste. The room was too hot, so of course she kept lifting up her arms and coiling her hair onto the top of her head as she chatted away, and then it would tumble down again, and she'd lift her arms once more.

'I'd better go…'

'Already?' Celeste said, but then they got talking, oh, just about this and that, and suddenly it was after ten. As he stood at the door to really go this time, Celeste found herself thinking that she'd had the nicest night in a long time.

Too nice, even.

Because of all the stupid things to be thinking, she was wondering what it would be like to be kissed goodnight by him.

Wondering what she'd do if that lovely mouth came a little bit closer.

'Thanks for the flowers, by the way.' Ben broke into her thoughts. 'You shouldn't have done that.'

'It's no problem.'

'No, you really shouldn't have done that.' Ben grinned. 'They'll be dead in two days—I'll forget to water them.'

'I won't.' Celeste smiled. 'Just enjoy.'

It was a relief to close the door on him!

CHAPTER FOUR

THEY ignored each other at work, of course.

Well, they didn't mention their evenings by the television or walks on the beach and sometimes as she sat in the staffroom and listened as Deb rattled on about how sure she was that Ben was going to ask her out (when Ben had already told her that he was embarrassed by Deb's constant flirting), or when the gorgeous Belinda started talking rather too warmly about him, though Celeste sat like a contended Buddha, inside she was fuming and could have cheerfully strangled them quiet.

She liked him.

Which was okay and everything. After all, half the department liked him in that way too, she was hardly in a minority—no, there was a slightly bigger problem than that.

Sometimes, *sometimes* she got that nervous fluttering feeling, which could only be generated by two.

Sometimes, *sometimes* she got this fleeting glimpse that Ben liked her too.

She told herself she was imagining it—as surely as

Deb was. Because there was no way Ben could possibly be interested in her.

So why was he acting so strangely?

Coffee break over, she headed back to Cots—and tried to tell her stupid heart to stop beating so quickly at the sight of him, except it didn't listen. It picked up speed half an hour later, only for different reasons as a rather frantic mother handed Celeste a very floppy baby.

She pushed on the call bell even before she unwrapped him.

He was big and chubby and barely opened his eyes as Celeste swiftly undressed him and ran some obs.

'He keeps vomiting…' The mum was trying not to cry. 'He saw the GP yesterday, she said it was gastro and to push fluids into him…'

No help was coming, so Celeste pushed the call bell again. The baby's pulse was racing and his temperature was high, so she put him on some oxygen and pushed the call bell *again* as she pulled over the IV trolley, resorting in the end to sticking her head out of the cubicle.

'Could I have a hand?' she snapped, and shot a frantic look at Ben, who was showing a patient his ankle X-ray. 'Now!'

'Press it three times for an emergency!" Ben snapped back, when he saw the baby.

She was still learning which way was up—only yesterday she had been warned for overreacting and pressing three times for everything remotely urgent and now she was being scolded for doing too little.

Some days this job was just so hard!

'Depressed fontanel.' Ben swiftly examined the listless baby, as Celeste quickly lifted him off the scales and set up for an IV. She was terrified of putting an IV line in such a sick baby, but it was part of her course and something she had to learn to do. She'd started on big, strapping, muscle-bound men with veins like tram lines, and then on sick adults. She had even put IVs in a few children now and a couple of babies as well, only not one as unwell as this and not with Mum anxiously watching—and now Meg was here too! 'Poor skin turgor.' Ben continued with his assessment then shook his head as he saw the slight shake of her hands as Celeste held the floppy arm with one hand and poised the needle with the other. 'I'll do it.' He took over without further comment and she was glad that he had. As a fat little baby, his veins would be hard to find at the best of times, but collapsed from dehydration they were proving extremely difficult and even Ben, with very steady hands, took a couple of goes to establish IV access, eventually finding a vein in his foot.

'I'm in.' He took some bloods and held the IV in firm place as Celeste connected it to a drip and then taped and wrapped it, carefully splinting his foot as Mum hovered close. As Ben relayed the IV fluids he wanted the babe to receive, he glanced up at Celeste with a quick addition. 'Could you put on a mask, please?'

She didn't see *him* putting on a mask, and neither was he asking Meg to. She gritted her teeth, for now she did as she was told. It was becoming an all too familiar pattern—in the couple of weeks that they had been working together Ben had become rather—for want of a word—annoying! She was already being looked out for by her colleagues and was uncomfortable enough with that, but Ben seemed to be on a mission to ensure that she saw only the safest, calmest, least infectious patients and if he wasn't suggesting that she put on a mask he was reminding her to wash her hands!

As if she needed reminding!

Still, with Ben now speaking with the mother, it was hardly the time or place for discussion—she'd save it for later.

'He's nine months old,' Ben checked with the anxious mum as Celeste sweated behind her mask. 'Is that right?'

'Only just nine months,' his mum said. 'I know he looks older.'

'How long as he been sick?' Ben asked.

'He started vomiting yesterday, three, maybe four times.'

'And this morning?' He fired questions as he continued to examine the baby and ordered a bolus dose of fluids for him. Celeste had already put him on oxygen and the paediatricians were on their way down, but Ben was examining his abdomen carefully, concerned that it was the surgeons that they needed. 'What colour is the vomit?'

'Green.'

'Okay…' He checked the baby's nappy and, still not happy with the abdomen, asked Meg to page the surgeons. Having spoken briefly with the mother, he rang Imaging to order an urgent ultrasound.

'I think it's an ileus,' Ben said, standing on hold on

the phone at the nurses' station as Celeste pointedly washed her hands at the little sink there, yet annoyingly as she dried her hands he pushed the bottle of alcohol hand rub towards her.

'Does that diagnosis mean I can go in there without a mask now?' Celeste asked, and then she frowned. 'Or is that suddenly an airborne disease too?' She watched his jaw tighten.

'You just need to be careful,' Ben pointed out. 'At that age, he could have measles, chickenpox, slap cheek…'

'Here.' He pushed the bottle of hand scrub to her again as she climbed onto the stool to write her notes, but she ignored it.

'You should use this,' he insisted.

'Why?' Celeste challenged.

'Because we don't know what's wrong with the baby yet, because you should—'

'Ben.' She clicked off her pen and put it down. 'While I appreciate your concern, I really don't need you to look out for me.'

'I'm not looking out for you—I'm just—'

'Making me paranoid!' Celeste said. 'Ben, I can beat you on the paranoid stakes with this pregnancy any day!'

He doubted that, but bit his tongue.

'I'm just ensuring that you take sensible precautions,' he said instead.

'I've spoken with my obstetrician, with the infectious diseases nurse, with Meg, and I'm using universal precautions. I'm being as sensible and as careful as possible, but dealing with sick people is part and parcel of nursing,' she said calmly.

'I don't see that it can hurt to take a few more precautions,' he muttered.

'I can't walk around in a spacesuit,' Celeste said, 'and neither can the nurses on the children's or oncology wards, neither can the nurses or radiographers who don't even know that they're pregnant but might be…' She could see his frown descending as the grad nurse gave the registrar a stern talking to. 'And all we can be is sensible, *all* the time, not just when we're visibly pregnant, so thank you for your concern and, no, I won't be using this…' she pushed back the bottle of alcohol scrub '…because I happen to be allergic to it.'

'Fine!' Ben snapped, more annoyed with himself than her. If her doctor was happy to let her keep working, and the hospital was still employing her, if Celeste wanted to keep working—well, it wasn't his concern.

So why was he so worried about her?

It niggled at him all day and later into the evening when, confused, he stood at the supermarket, basket in hand, and chose organic steak, because it was better for the baby—which, again, wasn't his concern, but he just stuffed it in his basket and added a carton of orange juice with added iron. He knew he was overreacting and he had every reason to. It was the anniversary of Jen's death in a couple of days, so it was no wonder he was upset. But then he did what he always did—and chose not to think about it.

A very vague routine had developed—not every day, not even every other day but now and then. He'd wander down and ask if she fancied dinner, or he'd hear her watering the sunflowers at his front door and pop his head around and ask her if she wanted to watch a movie, or whatever.

It was company, that was all.

And she was so-o-o glad of it.

So glad not to have to be as bright and bubbly as she pretended to be when she was at work—so nice to chat and moan, or sit with her feet up on his coffee table and watch a movie.

And never, not once, did he lecture her, or question her decision to keep working.

Till at the end of thirty-three weeks, till *that* night, when, full from organic steak and salad washed down with orange juice with added iron, she heaved herself off the sofa, and Ben glanced at his watch.

'It's only eight-thirty.'

'I just fancy an early night.'

'You're on a day off tomorrow.' Ben frowned, reluctantly seeing her to the door. His own company was the last thing he wanted over these next few nights. 'Are you sure you're okay?'

'I've got a doctor's appointment tomorrow. I want to—'

'Make sure that you look well rested, so you can fool him,' Ben said, and then stopped, his jaw muscles clamping, because it was *none* of his damn business what she did.

'I need to work for a few more weeks,' Celeste said, and Ben said nothing. He just forced a smile, and opened the door, telling himself that she didn't need a lecture, just a friend, but it was getting harder and harder to hold his tongue.

Then she burst into tears.

Celeste, who always smiled, always laughed, always came back with a quick retort, crumpled and gave in.

'I can't do it any more!'

All he felt was relief, relief that she'd seen it, relief that she wouldn't be doing it any more, and he pulled her, sobbing, into his arms and let her weep.

'Then don't,' he said gently.

'I can't afford not to,' she argued, but with herself now. 'Only I just can't face going there again…'

'I know.'

'I'm so tired.'

'I know.'

'And I'm scared of the germs too.'

'Come on.' He led her back to his sofa, fetched some cold water from the fridge and then gently he spoke with her, just as he would a patient, and explored her options. She had everything in place, even had some savings, but it would only just cover the rent and not much else. There would be a bit more money once the baby came along, but undoubtedly things were impossibly tight for her financially.

'The car's about to give up,' Celeste sobbed. 'And I haven't got a baby seat for it. I was going to get that with next month's pay…'

'My sister has had hundreds of car seats—the garage is full of them. She had twins…so that's sorted, okay?'

It was just the tip of a very big iceberg, just another thing on her endless list, but it was a relief to tick it off, to share, to finally admit just how drained from it all she really was.

'I need to work, but I really think that if I carry on,

it will affect the baby.' She was so glad that he didn't jump in and confirm her fears. 'I've got all this fluid…'

'Look.' Ben was supremely gentle. 'You've done well to get this far.'

'Some women work right to the end.'

'And some women don't,' Ben said. 'Some women can't, and it looks as if you're one of them.'

'I'll speak to the doctor tomorrow.' She nodded. 'I'll be honest.'

'Good,' Ben said, then he paused. And dived in where he didn't want to, got just a little bit more involved. 'Have you thought of asking the father for help?'

'Never.' Celeste shook her head. 'And please don't give me a lecture saying that he's responsible too, and that I've every right—'

'No lecture,' Ben interrupted. 'What about your parents?'

'I've written to them.' He realised how hard that would have been for her—knew from their chats how outraged their response had been, how they had cut her off. The fact that she had written and asked them for help after they'd done that to her showed she was thinking about the baby.

'Well done.'

It was the nicest thing he could have said. 'I only posted it yesterday, so I haven't heard. I've asked if I can move back, just for a few weeks…'

He'd miss her, Ben realised, but it was the right thing for her now. She needed family, needed someone to take care of her during these last difficult weeks—and it certainly wasn't going to be him.

'I'm going to speak to the doctor tomorrow.' Her voice was firmer now. 'And then I'll tell Meg.'

'Good.'

'And now…' again he pulled her up from the sofa as she went to stand '…I'm really going home to bed.'

He smiled at her as they reached the door. 'You'll get there,' Ben said, 'you really will.'

'I know.'

She was so tired and so weary and lost, trying to be brave in the dark, that this time when he pulled her into his arms, it wasn't because she was crying, it wasn't because she was upset. He didn't actually know why he'd done it, it just felt very right to hold her.

And for Celeste it felt so wonderful to *be* held for a moment.

A lovely, lovely moment to just stand and lean on him, to feel his words in her hair, his assurances that she had made the right choices, that she would be okay, and that she was doing well.

'I'm scared.'

She had never, not once, admitted it to anyone.

Defiance had become her middle name, because if she stopped for just a second, if she questioned her wisdom to keep the baby, to go on working, to not publicly name the father, to admit, even to herself, that she was struggling, then surely, *surely*, all the balls she was juggling would come clattering down. It was easier to cope, to insist she *was* coping, to just get on and do, rather than stop and think.

Yet in his arms she stopped for a moment—admitted the truth and waited for the crash.

Waited for the balls to clatter to the floor, for everything to grind to a halt, for hopelessness to invade, yet as she stood there, held by him, all she did was pause, just this blink of a pause where she told her truth and, safe for a moment, regrouped.

'Scared of what?' After the longest time he asked her.

'The baby deserves better.'

Ben closed his eyes in regret. Shameful regret because he had, at one time, thought the same too.

Two affluent parents, conceiving a baby that was planned, loved, wanted…

It had been his blueprint, his rage at the universe, because if he and Jen, with all they had, with all their plans and dreams, couldn't get there, why should anyone else?

Only now he held Celeste and realised that, despite the circumstances, the woman in his arms met the last two on the list and, despite the odds, she'd make up for all the rest.

'It's got *you*.' He stayed there, still holding her, and thought about it—thought how lucky that little baby was to have her, unplanned or whatever. It had Celeste—and he thought how she'd made him smile so many times, thought of the warmth of her affection and how lucky the recipient of that would be, and his neat blueprint faded from his mind.

'Am I enough, though?' she asked anxiously.

'Oh, yes,' he replied definitely.

She was absolutely enough.

More than enough.

So much more than enough, only he wasn't talking

about the baby now, because holding her, for the first time holding her, he forgot what they were talking about, forgot that she was pregnant. She was simply Celeste, funny, kind and terribly, terribly sexy. The scent of her up close, the soft feel of her head against his chest, overcame him, and he was lost in her. As naturally as breathing, he told her how he felt with a kiss instead of words, just pulling up her chin and kissing her. He lowered his head onto dark red lips and confirmed how *enough* she was with his mouth, and as their lips met Ben experienced this heady rush, like sugar dissolving on his tongue, as he tasted temptation.

She was stunned, because this was nothing like she had ever felt before, because in Ben's arms she felt safe, and just herself. Good, bad, whatever, she was herself with Ben. She had admitted to him that she was scared and the world had carried right on moving, only now it was even better than before.

His hands were in her hair and his mouth was moving with hers and she felt sexy—for the first time in her life she felt sexy and cherished and safe. And Ben felt it too, this tenderness and want rushing in that was *finally* without comparison. There was no logical thought to it—it was just a kiss, but one that tasted like heaven, surrounded by the scent of her hair and with her tongue cool from water. It was instinct, just the haven of instinct.

She kissed him back.

Kissed Ben in a way she never had before.

Not a practised kiss, not the type you have to think about—it was all about tasting, sharing, which was just how it should be. Ben's privacy, the isolated place that was him was suddenly hers to explore, and it tasted divine. Celeste had stepped inside the exclusive inner sanctum of this guarded man and she gloried in it.

'Celeste.' He groaned her name into her mouth, so she knew that she was there, knew she *was* the woman he was kissing tonight. One of his hands was on the back of her head, bringing her face to his, the other was on her bottom, her big fat dimply bottom, she vaguely thought, except he cupped it and stroked it till all it felt was fabulous. She hadn't really known what sexy was, yet she was discovering it now, right now, when it should be the last thing on her mind. Yet she was only a woman and, as his hands gathered her closer to him, it was all she wanted to be.

He had never come closer to escape—to a place where it was just him.

It wasn't a selfish escape.

Because also in that place was Celeste, and for a blissful few moments Ben was himself—the real him, the one that had been lost for ages. So he kissed her, tasted her, wanted her, without past or future, just succumbed to the heady taste of the present. He was hard, and he could feel her lovely bottom in his hands; he was in the place where bliss was no longer enough and then you reached for more, so he pulled her into his hardness, wanted to feel her softness against him, to shed her clothes, to drown in her. But instead he felt the solid weight of the baby that had been there only on the periphery of his mind now pressed into him. He could feel the dense weight of it and, tonight of all nights, it felt like a punch to the stomach, and it was Ben who pulled back.

'I'm sorry.' He released her so quickly it felt as if she were falling. 'That shouldn't have happened.'

Maybe it shouldn't have, but it had. It wasn't the kiss that embarrassed her—she was saving that for later. Right now it was his reaction—he was acting as though he was completely appalled at what he had done.

'Forget it…' She attempted casual, with a heart rate topping a hundred, as if shot awake from a blissful dream. Only now she was facing stark reality and just wanted out of there, as soon as she could. 'Really, it's no big deal.'

'Celeste…' Hell, he didn't want to add to her problems—only he just had, Ben knew that. But he had forgotten in that moment that she was pregnant. As he'd held her, all she had been was Celeste. 'Like I said, I'm not looking for—'

'I get it, Ben,' she interrupted. 'And neither am I. It was just a kiss, just…' She shrugged helplessly, because it had been so much more than just a kiss. She could still taste him on her lips, still feel the delicious crush of him holding her, and now he had taken it all away. 'Just one of those things that should never have happened. It doesn't change anything.'

CHAPTER FIVE

ONLY everything changed.

He saw her come into work around lunchtime the next day and speak with Meg. Trying to pretend nothing had happened, she gave him a quick smile as she passed. It had been a kiss between friends, Ben told himself, that had maybe got just a little out of hand. He was certain they could move on from it, so when a little while later he met her in the corridor, he asked how she was.

'Not bad.' She gave him a breezy smile. 'I'm officially on maternity leave.'

'How are you, Celeste?' Belinda clipped past on high heels and stopped to ask.

'I was just telling Ben that I've been signed off.' He could see it was with great effort she was maintaining that smile. 'So I guess I'll see you both when I'm a mum.'

There was a message for him in there, Ben knew it, and, feeling guilty, he was almost relieved to hear it. He was having trouble believing how stupid he'd been last night. She had enough on her plate without him messing things up, and a waif with a baby was the very last thing he needed right now.

'I hope she's okay,' Belinda said as Celeste waddled off.

'She will be now she's not working,' Ben answered.

'No.' Belinda gave a little shake of her head. 'I meant that I hope she'll be okay on her own with a baby.'

'She's not a teenager…' They were walking back to the office, and Ben was getting more and more irritated with Belinda's gloom. 'She'll be fine.'

'But, still, it isn't going to be easy. I wonder who the father is? I mean, she's never said, and surely he should be responsible for something…'

'How's your new man?' Ben rapidly changed the subject as they reached their office. 'Still going strong?'

'Paul's amazing,' Belinda sighed happily. 'We're going away this weekend.'

'I know.' Ben grinned. 'I'm covering for you.'

'His ex-wife's got the kids.'

'Have you met them yet?'

'God, no.' Belinda rolled her eyes as she sorted out some paperwork. 'The last thing I need is someone else's kids.'

It was the last thing Ben needed too.

Of all the stupid things to do… As they worked on in silence, Ben was silently brooding. Whether he liked it or not, he was involved with Celeste and her baby up to a point. He couldn't just stop going over to see her while she remained his neighbour…

'Here.' Belinda broke into his introspection. 'I've got something for you.'

Ben went over to the computer and had to laugh as

twenty or so female faces pouted back at him from an internet dating agency's website. 'I typed in your details and came up with all these possibilities for you.'

'I'm not interested in dating, and certainly not this way,' he said.

'Oh, get into the twenty-first century.' Belinda laughed. 'At least you know what you're getting this way—I haven't got time to go out to the clubs. And I know Paul's not looking for a stay-at-home surrogate mother for his children—he knows from the start that my career comes first and I absolutely don't want a baby. Look, she's nice.' She brought up a woman's details and Ben read on.

'She says she wants someone with no baggage,' Ben pointed out. 'I've got a truckload.'

'We all have.' Belinda shrugged. 'You just have to lie a little. I mean, if you get to our age and have had any semblance of a life, baggage is the norm. Go on, Ben,' she urged. 'Give it a go.'

'Leave it, Belinda,' he warned. Colleagues he could deal with, friendly colleagues even, but Belinda was pushing the line. She was in love and hanging off lamp-posts and wanted to spread her happiness—but she was talking to the wrong guy. 'I couldn't be less interested in starting a relationship now.'

He meant it.

Four years ago tomorrow… He lay on the bed when he got home and closed his eyes.

Four years…

Had it been that long? It seemed like only yester-day—yet it had also stretched on for ever.

Four years... He snapped his eyes open suddenly, knowing that he just had to deal with the present problem that was Celeste before he could get on with remembering and mourning the past.

'I was wondering...' His voice trailed off. It had taken him ages to decide how best to deal with this and finally he had decided to drop by her place, to pretend nothing had happened, and then offer his solution. Except she had taken for ever to answer the door and when she did, it was clear that he had woken her up. There was a huge pillow crease down the side of her face and the usually sunny Celeste was decidedly grumpy and certainly not about to make this easy. 'Were you asleep?'

'Actually, yes, I was.'

'Sorry.' Ben cleared his throat. He didn't want to just drop helping her, but he did want to pull back and this might just be the way! 'I've got a day off tomorrow. I'm going to do a big shop because I'm having too many take-aways, and I wondered if you wanted to make a list. I could grab some stuff for you.'

'I'm fine, thanks.'

'It really is no problem. You said you were struggling to get to the shops—'

'I did my shopping this afternoon online,' Celeste interrupted. 'So I'm all right. I've got a friend coming over tomorrow and we're going to make a load of meals and stock up the freezer.'

'That's...great.'

'And the doctor said that I needed to rest a lot,' Celeste continued, 'so, I don't mean to sound rude, but…' she gave an uncomfortable swallow '…I'm having a lot of trouble getting to sleep, and I'd just nodded off when you knocked.'

'Sorry about that,' he apologised.

'You weren't to know.' She gave a slight smile, only it didn't reach her eyes, and neither did her eyes meet his. 'But it might be better if you don't…' she gave a tight shrug '…just drop over in future.'

'Sure,' Ben said. He should have been relieved. After all, he'd been hoping for the same thing. He was absolved from duty now, so why didn't it feel great? 'What did the doctor say?' he asked, not able to leave it there.

'I told you.' Celeste's usually sunny face was a closed mask. 'I'm to rest… Look, Ben, it's really not your concern.'

Then she closed the door.

He went back to his unit.

And as he had done for the last few years on this night, Ben tried and failed not to watch the clock.

The horrible thing about anniversaries, Ben had found, was the build-up to them—as if you were stuck in a portal, as if by somehow going over and over every detail, you could change the outcome, bargain with God.

Only not this night.

Oh, he did all that, but there was another layer there too.

Guilt.

Guilt, because when he surely should have been drowning his sorrows in whisky and thinking only of Jen, when he should surely be lacerating himself with thoughts of what could have been, this year he couldn't sustain it.

Instead, he found himself standing at the window and wondering about Celeste.

Found himself thinking not about what could have been, but what already was.

And what could be?

Time did heal.

He'd been told it, had said it himself, but only now was he actually starting to believe it.

It didn't consume him now, it didn't walk with him constantly, there was room in his mind for other thoughts, so on a day that was usually spent locked in mourning, he awoke, showered and dressed, went to the cemetery and told them he loved them—always had, always would—but instead of heading to her parents' home, instead of stopping, he started. He kept his appointment with the bank, saw the real-estate agent, looked around the house again, put a deposit on a boat, went home, saw that his sunflowers were dying, watered them, showered again, and got changed into shorts.

He did really well, actually!

Until Jen's parents rang.

And then so too did his.

Followed by Jen's sister.

And then it all finally caught up with him.

He tried not to look at the clock, tried not to remember ringing her from work, then tried to remember the *exact* tone of her voice when Jen had said she had a headache.

It had done nothing to alert him.

Well, actually it had, but he was a doctor and his wife was pregnant and also a doctor and between them they could dream up a million and one scenarios if they so wished. So she had told him it was just a headache…and he had told himself the same.

'It's just a headache, Ben.'

Except when he suggested that she take something for it, instead of her usual rebuff, he'd been concerned to find out that she already had. Jen, who never took anything, had taken a couple of painkillers.

'I'll come home,' he'd suggested.

'For God's sake, Ben.' She'd sounded irritated. 'It's a headache, I'm just going to go and lie down.'

Yes, by early evening it had all caught up with him again.

He didn't walk along the beach today, and he didn't jog. He ran. Only the beach seemed too small—he could see Melbourne miles away in the sunset, but he felt as if he could make it in a few leaps, that he would never run out of energy, that he could run all his life and still never leave it behind.

He wasn't wearing a watch, but he knew the time, knew it to the very second.

Ringing Jen and getting no answer, and telling himself she was just lying down.

He pounded the beach. His lungs were bursting but still, *still* he remembered walking up the garden path and trying not to run, because he was surely being stupid, because there was surely nothing wrong, then letting himself in and calling her name. It was five past seven, as he ran, Ben knew that, because suddenly he felt like swearing at the sky for cheating them, five past seven because he'd seen it on the clock as he had walked into the lounge, seen her kneeling on the floor, her hands on her head on the sofa.

So still.

So pale.

So gone.

Pounding on her chest, ringing the ambulance.

He wanted her and if not he wanted a Caesarean—he wanted life to be salvaged from the wreckage he had come home to, except he knew, knew, knew even as he laid her flat on her back that it was too late.

He ran along that beach, not as if the devil was chasing him, because nothing could catch him now. He was the chaser, pounding on anger, and regret and hate and the unfairness of it all.

Temper split his mind.

He didn't want Celeste and her baby.

He wanted *his*!

It was a relief to be off work, but it was also the longest, loneliest time.

Her request to stay at her parents' was met with a curt letter of refusal and a cheque, which Celeste would love to have not cashed on principle, but she couldn't afford principles right now. Although she'd have loved to splurge and get her hair cut and buy something fantastic and non-essential for the baby, instead she trimmed her hair with the kitchen scissors, bought another two boxes of nappies and paid two months' rent in advance, then crawled back into bed and carried on missing Ben.

And she did miss him.

Missed him more than she had Dean. Which made no sense, but it was how it was. Over and over she took out the memory of his kiss and explored it, remembered the moment that had ended them—and she wished she'd never tasted him, never been held by him, had never kissed him, because in that moment she'd glimpsed a different world. With just one kiss he'd shown her how good life could be—and then he'd ripped it away.

She thought about ignoring the knock at the door—but not for long. Maybe it was her parents to say they'd changed their minds, or the postman, or maybe, just maybe…

It was Ben.

'I hope I didn't wake you,' he said.

'You didn't.'

'And I'm sorry to drop round…' His four-wheel drive was purring behind him, the engine still going, no doubt ready to make a quick escape.

'It's fine.'

Ben wasn't finding this easy. The whole day hadn't been easy, in fact—but it was something he had promised, something he had to do. 'I went over to my sister's to get the car seat for you.'

'Oh!'

'Look.' He ran a hand through his hair. 'I don't want to offend you, so say if you don't want them, really, you just have to say. But she gave me a few things…a crib, a stroller, one of those jogging ones…'

'Do I have to promise to take up jogging?' she asked.

'No…' Despite the strained circumstances, she still made him smile.

'Only I might get challenged under the Trade Descriptions Act if I'm seen with it,' she teased.

'It's good for walking on the beach too,' Ben said. 'Well, according to my sister.'

She couldn't joke any more, really she didn't know what to say. It wasn't a question of being too proud to accept help, it was more that she'd had none, well, apart from her parents' cheque. But this was real help and real thought and that it came from him made it as bitter as it was sweet.

'Thank you,' she said sincerely.

'Do you want me to bring it in?' He gestured to the vehicle behind him and she said thank you again, her nose a bit red from trying not to cry.

She offered to help, but he shooed her away and she sat on the sofa as a lot of wishes were granted—just not the one she wished for the most, because he couldn't even look at her, Celeste noticed. Oh, he was kind and helpful and set up the crib and accepted a glass of iced tea while Celeste opened bag after bag, smiling at teeny tiny baby socks.

For Ben it was a nightmare.

All these things had been promised for him and Jen—the crib he was setting up now he hadn't got to do four years ago. The little socks and vest Celeste was holding up made him sweat, and even driving here had been hard, with an empty baby seat in the back...

Still, she needed it and he never would—it was stupid to let it go to waste and he had promised her the car seat that night.

That night.

'I'll leave you to it, then,' he said gruffly. It was almost more than he could stand to be in the room, surrounded by baby things, her home set up and almost ready now…almost more than he could stand to look at her, because she looked *terrible*!

So terrible, in fact, that he wanted to scoop her up and run—wanted someone to notice just how unwell this woman was. Where the hell were her parents?

'Did you hear from your mum and dad?'

'Yes.' She tried for upbeat but didn't manage to come close. 'They sent some money…' He could see her red nose, see the swirl of tears in her eyes despite the smile.

'And when…' Ben cleared his throat '…do you see your obstetrician again?'

'Next Wednesday!'

It was only Friday.

'When did you see him last?'

'On Tuesday.' Still the smile remained, but it was wavering now. 'If my blood pressure is still up they're going to admit me.'

'No protein in your urine?'

'No protein…' He was trying to be a doctor, trying to assess her practically, only it wasn't working. He knew they would be carefully monitoring her for pre-eclampsia, knew she was being watched, only he wanted her watched more closely, and as coolly as he tried to assess the facts, detachment wasn't working.

'You've got a lot of fluid, Celeste,' he pointed out.

'I know. I'm allowed one gentle walk a day, and I've cut out salt as well as sugar… They're watching me, Ben.'

And with that he had to make do.

Only he couldn't.

'Why don't you ring and get your appointment brought forward? I could take you there now,' he offered.

'Ben,' Celeste interrupted, 'thank you for all the lovely things—and thank you to your sister too. When I'm able, I'll get her a card.'

And with *that* he had to make do.

CHAPTER SIX

'HI CELESTE!' He gave a tight smile as she came over. The whole street had come out to watch the auction and Celeste had bypassed her gentle walk on the beach today and wandered down for a look—it was what people in Melbourne did on a sunny Saturday afternoon when a house was up for auction.

'Hi.' She was polite and said hello and then bypassed him, but Ben halted her.

'You're supposed to be resting.'

'I'm walking around a house instead of a beach!' Celeste pointed out. 'Anyway, I've got cabin fever. I'm going crazy being stuck inside the unit and at least they'll have the air-conditioning on in the house.' And then she gave him a smile. 'Thanks for yesterday, by the way.'

'No problem. I'm glad it's all going to good use.'

'I meant the doctor pep talk. I rang my obstetrician and they're seeing me on Monday now.'

'That's wonderful.'

'I'm going home to pack my case after this—I have a feeling they won't be letting me out.'

Then she moved on, wandered inside with the rest of

the crowd, and when Ben's eyes should have been on the competition, instead they were on her.

He wanted her.

As he walked around the house, stared into rooms, walked through the garden. It was Celeste's comments he wanted, not the real-estate agent's, and she gave plenty.

It *was* stunning. Her entire unit could fit neatly in the lounge, and Celeste was quite sure that if she could just lie on that lovely white sofa and gaze out at the water till Monday, with someone peeling grapes for her and massaging her feet, her blood pressure would be down by her doctor's appointment!

She loved viewing houses, wandering around them, pretending they were hers, and wishing it could be so. The kitchen was a hell-hole, though, but the agent steered them past it quickly and on to view the upstairs. The whole place was to die for—every room in the house, even the master bathroom, was angled for water views!

'There are no blinds,' Celeste pointed out, and Ben smothered a smile, because when he'd first looked around the home, he'd said exactly the same thing, only the agent hadn't ignored him! 'How can you have floor-to-ceiling windows in a bathroom and no blinds?' Celeste demanded.

'The glass is treated,' the agent hissed. 'You can see out, but no one can see in.

'Now, moving along, this is the master bedroom!'

'Divine!' Celeste breathed as she stepped in. A vast bed was in the centre, and there was a balcony set up with a little table and chairs…

'Are the windows treated in here too?' Celeste asked pointedly as the agent sucked in his breath.

She *did* make him smile.

And he *did* miss her.

She was writing on her little list again—just as if she was a serious bidder—and he could see the real-estate agent's lips purse as she stepped out boldly onto the balcony instead of following the pack back along the hall. 'Can you keep up, please?' the agent snapped, and Ben felt his teeth grind together.

'This room would make an ideal nursery…' Despite her obvious condition the agent addressed a loving young couple and ignored Celeste when she asked a question. How she wished she'd won the lottery, and could pull out the winning bid just to wipe that superior smile off his smug face and make him squirm. Ben saw her face redden as the agent ignored her and then caught her eye and gave her a wink.

'My partner asked a question,' Ben said coolly, watching Celeste's beam of delight as the agent practically gave himself whiplash, turning to face her. No, she hadn't won loads of money, but watching that smug smile leave his face was almost as good.

'I'm so sorry,' he simpered. 'What did you want to know?'

'Thanks for that.' Celeste grinned at Ben as they wandered outside.

'Ooh, it was my pleasure,' Ben replied. 'He's obnoxious.'

Celeste loved auctions—the crowd gathered outside the house, the real-estate agent pumping up the action—

yet she was always scared she'd put up her hand and outbid someone, like standing on the edge of a cliff and wanting to jump, just to try it.

There was some serious bidding going on, and Celeste watched on in glee. This was the most exciting thing to have happened to her all week.

Ben was trying to concentrate, but his eyes kept wandering to her.

He hadn't put in a bid yet—he would wait and see... God, even her eyelids were swollen. When he should be concentrating, when he should be focusing, instead he was thinking about her, worrying about her—and Ben didn't like the feeling a bit.

The bidding was slowing down now, the auctioneer having trouble eking out even a small raise in bids—and it was then that Ben put in his first offer.

He saw the flare of surprise in her eyes—she'd had no idea that he would be bidding. It wasn't something he had to discuss with anyone, Ben told himself, that was the life he had built for himself. Yet still there was a little pang of discomfort, remembering all the nights when she had spoken about her hopes and fears and dreams for the future, and he realised that he hadn't let her in at all.

The flagging crowd was suddenly interested, and Ben saw her smile. Just a little smile that winged its way over to him, telling him she was pleased.

Excited for him, even.

He was outbid, so he upped his offer.

And again she smiled.

He was outbid again, so he upped it again.

He looked over for her smile, for that bit of encouragement that he shouldn't need but somehow liked, and then he saw she wasn't smiling.

He had been outbid again, the auctioneer passing the bid to him, only Ben wasn't listening.

There was an aghast expression on Celeste's face, as if she had just received some shocking news—only there was no one talking to her and she wasn't on the phone. Her hands were both on her stomach.

He could hear the auctioneer's warning. Confused, but also needing to get over to her, Ben put in a ridiculously high bid, heard the gasp of shock from the crowd. Ignoring the rest of the proceedings, he waded through the crowd towards her.

'I think my waters just broke!'

'It's okay,' he said soothingly.

'No, it's not.' She was shivering, shock setting in as realisation hit. 'I'm only thirty-four weeks.'

'Thirty-four-weekers do very well…' He could hear his calm voice, only the blood was pounding in his temples as he pulled out his phone. 'Come on, let's get you sitting down. I'll call an ambulance.'

'There's nowhere to sit!' she shrilled. The sun was suddenly hot on her head, her mouth filling with saliva. 'Ben, I think it's coming…'

The real-estate agent had come over to congratulate him, the house apparently his now, but Ben wasn't listening.

'We need to get her inside,' he stated.

'Excuse me?' the agent said.

'Ben…' She was moaning now, whimpering in terror. 'I've got pain…'

'She needs to be inside.' Ben was walking her to the entrance at the side of the house, taking her weight. 'She needs some privacy…'

'You can't just go in!'

'I just bought the house!' Ben snapped. 'She's about to give birth. Where do you want her to do it—on the street?' He gave up walking her then and picked her up—and such was his authority that the real-estate agent actually opened the side gate for him. 'Now, call an ambulance,' Ben ordered, 'and tell them it's a premature baby…' He had her beneath the willow tree now and she was wriggling out of his arms, already starting to strain. Ben realised with alarm that there was no chance of getting her inside. 'And say there's a doctor in attendance.'

'Is there anything I can do?' The man he had waved to each morning, the man he had just bought a house from, was now there, being practical and helpful. 'Some towels,' Ben said as his wife rushed off and he struggled to be calm, to be professional. It was a delivery, he told himself, he was more than capable of dealing with that. Only he could see her terrified eyes…

'I need you to listen to me, Celeste.' He had pulled down her panties and examined her. The baby wasn't waiting for the ambulance, it wasn't waiting for anything… 'This *is* a small baby, so we're going to try and slow it down.' It was important that they did so, as a rapid delivery could cause damage to the fragile brain. 'You're not to push,' he warned Celeste. 'We want this to happen as slowly and as gently as we can…'

She had never been more petrified—the thought of her baby coming so soon and here, no hospital, no shiny equipment… Yet she was suddenly desperate to bear down, to push, only Ben was telling her to just breathe through it, to resist this desperate urge—and she knew why. 'It's too fast…'

'Your body will have been preparing for this for hours, you just didn't know.' He smiled. 'We just need to slow down this last bit.'

He was right. All morning she had felt restless— trying to lie in bed, to read, to rest. She'd had a shower and then gone back to bed, then decided to go and look at the auction…

'It's coming,' she moaned.

It was. Nothing was going to slow down her baby's entrance to the world, and she was so glad Ben was here and terrified that he might not have been.

'What if I'd been at home, what if…?'

'You'd have coped!' Ben cut short her what-ifs. 'And you're coping well now.'

'I'm sorry we're not talking.' She panted with the effort of not pushing. 'I'm sorry to do this to you…'

'I'm glad to be here,' Ben said, 'I've done this pl—' He didn't continue, as he'd just seen that the cord was around the neck, but not tightly, and he slipped it over. Only it wasn't just that which had halted his words. Yes, he had delivered babies over the years, yes, he had done this plenty of times before.

Just not like this.

Not like this, with his heart in his mouth, as he held a tiny head in his hand and guided a pale life into the world.

Not like this, as he delivered the babe onto Celeste's stomach, rubbed at its back, flicked at its feet. He knew it would breathe, the doctor in him knew that it had only been a minute, but for Ben it was one very long minute, the babe floppy and cyanosed, its heart rate tipping almost low enough that if it went down further he would have to commence CPR. He could hear Celeste's pleas and they matched his thoughts, willing the ambulance faster with oxygen for this little one. He turned the baby over, its back now on Celeste's stomach, and felt his head lighten in relief as the tiny baby startled and took its first breath.

'It's not crying,' Celeste sobbed.

'She will,' he promised.

'She?' Ben was no midwife—maybe it should have been for mum to find out herself, except the baby was too fragile and sick for anything other than practicality.

'You've got a daughter,' Ben said, 'and she needs to be kept warm.' He kept the little one on her mother's stomach, and wrapped them both in towels, relieved to finally hear the sirens.

'I got some string….' The woman who had got the towels had been busy and had the ambulance not been pulling up Ben would have cut the cord then. He was seriously worried at the babe's lack of response. She was breathing, but with effort, little bubbles coming out of her mouth with each breath. The paramedics were straight onto it—suctioning her little airway, even the tiniest oxygen mask swamping her tiny features as Ben clamped and cut the cord.

'We might radio through…' The paramedic looked at Ben, a quick decision being made between them without words—to attempt IV access and work to stabilise her here, or to scoop and run and get her to the hospital which was just a short drive away, depending on the traffic?

'Let's get her to hospital,' Ben said, and the paramedic nodded, wrapping her up in towels.

'We'll send another vehicle for Mum,' the paramedic said.

'No, I want to go with her…' Celeste was sobbing, shivering and shaking, stunned at the speed of it all.

'She needs to get to hospital quickly.' Ben's voice was kind but non-negotiable. 'Can you stay with Celeste for a moment?' He spoke with the woman who had been so helpful. She had brought pillows and blankets from the house now and was doing her best to make Celeste comfortable. 'I'm going to help them get the baby settled in the ambulance and then I'll be back.'

'No,' Celeste sobbed. 'Go with her. Please.'

There was a flash of confusion at his own thought process then, only he didn't pursue it—there wasn't time. He nodded his acquiescence and held the infant as the ambulance sped them the short distance to the hospital. Her little lungs were filling up with fluid and Ben held the oxygen mask close to her face, but allowing room for the paramedic to suction. There was a little probe attached to her ear and her oxygen saturation was low but not dire…

The ambulance swept through the streets, slowing down at High Street, which was filled with Saturday shoppers and weekend drivers, and Ben felt his tension rising as it braked and accelerated, the siren blasting out.

Then he looked beyond the mask and the flaring nostrils and he saw the creamy vernix-flattening dark curls, and navy eyes that were nowhere near able to focus, except he felt as if she was looking straight at him.

It was a bizarre moment of connection, and it was Ben who tore his eyes away first.

He was only the doctor.

This baby's mother was just a friend...

Then the hospital was in view, and he could see Belinda waiting outside. As the ambulance opened he didn't hand the little one over, but ran inside to Resus with the precious bundle—the resuscitation cot warmed and waiting, paediatricians and Raji there, and only then did he hand her over...

And only then did he realise how terrified he had been. A cold sweat was drenching him as he saw the urgency in the assembled staff, and he knew that this was no overreaction. He saw how very sick this little baby was and he was unable to speak for a moment as he struggled to get his breath.

He headed over to the sink as the paramedics gave the handover, and Ben took a long drink directly from the tap, before walking back to where they were working.

Raji had placed a tube down her nose and was suctioning her airway more deeply, the paediatrician had just inserted an umbilical line and fluids were now being delivered. She looked a touch more feisty than she had, her face scrunching in displeasure, little fists bunching and legs kicking a small protest...

'She was very flat...' Ben gave the Apgar scores. 'It was a very rapid delivery.'

'Thirty-four weeks, the paramedics said.' The paediatrician was looking her over. 'But she's quite big for thirty-four weeks—do you know where mum was having her antenatal?'

'I'm sure he didn't have time to ask,' Belinda said. 'You were at a house auction, weren't you, Ben?'

'Actually...' he cleared his throat a touch '...this is Celeste's baby.'

'*Our* Celeste!' Belinda blinked and then looked at the admission card that the receptionist had just filled in. 'Baby Mitchell...'

'She lives in the same street as the auction,' Ben half explained, 'and she must have wandered down to watch it.'

'Well, lucky woman...' Belinda breathed out '...that you were there.'

'She had gestational diabetes,' Ben said, which explained the baby's relatively big size for gestation, 'and she had her antenatal care here,' he added to the receptionist, and she rushed off to get the notes.

'Does anyone know if there were any other problems?'

'Hypertension,' Meg said as still Ben struggled just to breathe. 'She was signed off a couple of days ago.'

'Her blood pressure has been up,' Ben said, watching Belinda blink at the depth of his knowledge. 'She looked very bloated today, and I thought she was tipping into pre-eclampsia,' Ben added. 'I think she was going to be admitted on Monday.'

He felt sick.

The resuscitation area was impossibly hot, and Ben felt stifled, hearing the blip, blip, blip of the monitor. Even watching the team at work was incredibly hard. Oh, he knew they knew what they were doing, knew that babies were tough, even tiny ones, only they seemed so rough with their handling of something so very, very small.

'I'm going to go outside for a bit,' Ben said in a strangled voice.

'You might want to change first.' Belinda glanced up and smiled and only then did Ben register the state he was in.

He had a quick shower and selected some theatre blues, only instead of drying and dressing he sat on the wooden bench, dripping wet, with his head in his hands, her words playing over and over. *'What if I'd been at home, what if…?'* Scenario after possible scenario was playing out in his racing brain.

And not just for this morning.

Over and over the years he had beaten himself up with those very words—wishing he'd come home earlier, wondering about the outcome if he had. He'd been told that nothing could have been done for Jen, that even with the best of care she'd have died, or worse, that the brain haemorrhage she'd suffered would have left her a vegetable. But what about their baby? Could it have been saved if he'd been at home?

There was a myriad of conflicting emotions pelting him.

Relief, regret, resentment even, that he had been there for this child and not his own—and yet, even as resentment flickered it faded just as quickly. That tiny life he had held in his hands, he had willed and willed to live, had felt more for than a doctor should—and not just for the baby, but for her mother too.

Then he remembered his own stupidity, that he had contemplated staying with her after the traumatic birth of her baby.

Of course he should have gone with the baby!

Celeste was stable, another ambulance on the way... and yet instinct had overridden logic for a second, and all he had wanted to do was stay and comfort her.

No!

He stood up then and dried quickly, pulling on his theatre blues and making a firm decision. He wasn't going to get involved with Celeste—whatever it took.

He just couldn't go there again.

Wouldn't.

Couldn't.

CHAPTER SEVEN

'WHEN can I see her?' It was *all* she could think about.

The ambulance had arrived a couple of moments after they had taken her daughter, and she had been taken directly to Maternity. The midwives had been wonderful, keeping her up to date on her baby's progress as Celeste was examined and an IV inserted and bloods taken.

'Why do I need that?'

'Your blood pressure's still high,' the obstetrician explained, 'and you've got a lot of fluid retention. We just want to check your bloods and keep an eye on you, make sure everything's settling down…'

The midwives helped her to wash and freshen up and get into bed and then Gloria, who Celeste had guessed was the one in charge, finally came in with some real news.

'They've just transferred her from Emergency to Special Care. Once they've got her settled and as soon as *your* doctor gives you the okay, we'll take you over to see her. Here.' She handed her a photo. 'One of the nurses took this…'

Oh, she was tiny, with a little pink hat and tubes and things everywhere, but she *was* hers… The few moments she'd had with her daughter were imprinted on her mind and Celeste already recognised her, could walk into the special care unit now and pick out her daughter, of that she was positive…

'Now,' Gloria said, 'she's doing well, and she's on CPAP. That just means she's needing a little help with her breathing, to fill her lungs with air, and she's been given surfactant and medicines to help with lung immaturity…' She went through all the treatment her daughter was receiving till Celeste understood and then she *again* asked a necessary question, one that Celeste had so far refused to respond to. 'Is there anyone we can call for you?' Celeste shook her head.

'I'll ring my parents soon.'

'You shouldn't be on your own,' Gloria said gently. 'Is there a friend…?'

'Later.' Again, Celeste shook her head.

She wanted some privacy, didn't want to share this moment now with parents who hadn't helped, who apart from a terse phone call and a single cheque had done nothing. And neither did she want friends who hadn't really been there around her, or a father who didn't want to know—all of that she would face and deal with, but right now she just wanted to process all that had taken place by herself…

'Hey!' The door opened and Ben's face appeared. He was perhaps the one person she didn't mind seeing right now—after all, he had been there!

'Thank you.' How paltry it sounded, but she meant it from her heart.

'You're very welcome.'

'How is she?'

'I'm not sure,' Ben said. 'They moved her from Emergency half an hour or so ago…'

'Oh!' Of course he wouldn't know, Celeste told herself. As if he followed his patients up to the ward! Once he had handed the baby over, that would have been it for him.

'How are you doing?' Ben asked.

'Not bad…' She didn't elaborate, didn't want to bore him with the tests she was having. He was asking politely, that was all.

'Well…' he gave a tight smile '…I can't stay. I've got the real-estate ringing every five minutes—I need to sign the contract on the house.'

'You'd better go, then.'

'Do you need anything?'

'No.'

'If you need me to drop by the unit I can fetch some stuff. Do you have a bag packed?'

'No.' Celeste gave a weak smile. 'I'm not that organised. Could I ask you just to check the plugs and things?' she asked reluctantly, when he clearly just wanted out of there. 'I think everything is off, but I only went out for a walk.'

'Sure.' He handed over her handbag, which was on her locker, and waited while she gave him her keys. 'Anything else?'

'Nothing I can think of.'

'Well, I'm on a night shift tonight, so I'll drop these back to you.' And even though he was taking her keys, even though he would be going back to her flat and checking her things, his voice, his stance was as formal as if he were just another doctor doing rounds. 'Congratulations, Celeste.'

'Thank you.'

It was an exhausting evening.

There was no rosy glow of motherhood for Celeste to bathe in. She told her parents the news and as expected they arrived a couple of hours later, bringing with them their endless questions and practically blaming her for the stress they were under.

'What were you doing, walking?' her mother Rita scolded her. 'You were supposed to be resting.'

'The doctor said that I was allowed a gentle walk each day.'

'Have you rung him?' Rita asked. 'Whoever *he* is. Have you let him know he's a father?'

'No.'

'Well, don't you think you should? It is *his* responsibility…'

The time or place didn't matter. The same arguments that had ensued since the day she had told them she was pregnant carried on at the hospital bedside. So much for a baby bringing peace, Celeste thought, waving goodbye to the fantasy that the arrival of their grandchild would cast the arguments aside.

'When will we get to see her?' Rita demanded as Gloria came in.

'It's just Mum allowed in for now,' Gloria said, seeing Celeste's strained face. 'They're ready for you, Celeste.'

It was a relief to be wheeled out of the room and away from them.

'You can actually have one of them come in with you,' Gloria said once they were out of earshot. 'If you want—'

'No,' Celeste interrupted. 'I'd rather see her on my own first.'

They had to sit in a little annexe for a few moments until they were ready for them.

'You poor thing.' Gloria gave her a kind smile, as they sat there. 'I bet this is so not how you planned it.'

'None of it's how I planned it,' Celeste admitted.

'You are allowed to cry, you know.' Gloria put her arm around Celeste's shoulders and felt her stiffen. 'It's been such a difficult day…' Celeste wriggled away because if she started crying she wouldn't stop.

And then it was time… She was wheeled in to wash her hands, and then she was wheeled past the incubators and finally she got to see her daughter.

Lying like a little washed-up frog with all drips and tubes and that little pink hat on… Even then she couldn't cry, couldn't give in, because she felt she had to be responsible, so she listened instead as the special care nurse explained all the drips and tubes and that her daughter was comfortable…

'Can I hold her?' Celeste asked, when they didn't offer.

'Not today. We're keeping her very quiet for now, but probably tomorrow…'

So she got to hold her fingers instead and stared at her teeny pink nails and waited for this whoosh of love to come. It was there a little bit, only it wasn't exactly whooshing as she'd expected—because there was this huge plug of guilt lodged in its way.

'Have you got a name for her?'

'Not yet,' Celeste said. 'I wanted to see what she looked like.' She gazed at her daughter and tried to think of a name that might suit her, but her brain was too fuddled for such a big decision. 'I don't know.'

'There's plenty of time,' Gloria said. 'We should get you back—you're not well either, remember.'

She wasn't.

The obstetrician came in and explained that her blood tests had come back and the results weren't great. 'They should all settle over the next few days now that you've delivered, but we will need to keep an eye on you. You've got pre-eclampsia, Celeste.'

'Had.' Celeste frowned. 'Doesn't it go away once the baby is here?'

'Not straight away,' he explained. 'You're still quite sick. You were being observed for it as your blood pressure was raised at your last antenatal, but…well, you had a lot of other stresses that could have accounted for that. It's good that you've delivered. It could have been dangerous for you both had the pregnancy continued.'

It was a long, lonely evening—friends came and visited, but it was as if they were speaking a foreign language. Oh, they cooed and oohed at the photos, but when eight o'clock came and they headed out for Saturday night, Celeste just lay there with her eyes closed, not because she was tired but because she was scared she'd cry. She ignored the footsteps coming into the room, they could take her blood pressure without talking, and then she heard her keys being placed on the locker and screwed them closed more tightly.

Ben could see a tear slipping out of the side of one eye, and could only hazard a guess as to how hard this day had been for her.

He knew he should just put down the bag and walk out quietly. After all, he had resolved not to get involved—a young single mum was the last thing he needed. She was so young and fragile and he was so jaded and bitter, and his heart was closed so tightly. Only sometimes she managed to wedge it open a little…

'I know you're awake!' Reluctantly he broke the silence, smiling a little at her defiant answer.

'I'm not.'

'I packed a few things for you—your toothbrush and hairbrush…'

'Thanks.'

'Is there anything else you need—a nightdress or anything?'

'No, thanks,' she answered, her eyes still closed. 'Mum said she'd go shopping tomorrow.'

'How were they?' Ben asked, even as he told himself he shouldn't, looking up at the diuretic infusion and the magnesium infusion and then back to her poor, swollen face.

'Cross.' More tears were spilling out the sides of her eyes now, and he picked off a few tissues and put them in her hand. 'They're still cross with me.'

'They're worried,' Ben said.

'And cross,' Celeste said. 'And so are you.'

'Cross?' Ben frowned. 'Celeste, why would I be

cross…?' His voice faded as her eyes opened to him, because she was right. Cross was how he felt—or was he just worried?

He truly didn't know.

'Because we kissed…because you think I just go around flinging myself at men—'

'No,' Ben interrupted, 'I'm not cross at you for that, I'm cross with myself.'

'Why?'

'Because…' He blew out a breath, and he couldn't help but admire her for being so open, for just bringing it out. He sat on the bed, because he definitely wasn't a doctor dropping in now. 'Because I'm the last thing you need right now.'

'You don't know what I need.'

'You don't need *me*,' Ben said very firmly, very surely. 'Since Jen, I've had a few relationships and they don't work. You've been messed around enough without getting involved with someone like me, someone who doesn't want children…'

'You think I'm after a father for her?' Celeste asked incredulously. 'Some long-term commitment from you? Hell, Ben, it was only one kiss!'

'That shouldn't have happened,' Ben said.

'I know,' Celeste admitted. He was right, absolutely he was right. 'You're wrong about one thing, though,' she challenged. 'I'm not after a relationship. I'm having enough trouble getting used to being a mum without someone else in the picture. It's bad enough that her own father…' She started to cry then because she couldn't believe how wrong she'd got it, that the man she had thought she was in love with had thought so very little of her.

'Have you told him?' And he said it in such a different way from the way her mum had—not accusing. He just asked the question and watched her face crumple.

'I rang just before you came…'

'And?'

'He doesn't want to know.'

'I'm so sorry,' he said gently.

'I'm not,' Celeste sniffed. 'Well, I am for her, but not for me. At least I know where I stand. I will be okay on my own, you know!'

'I know that,' he said with a small smile at her vehemence.

'And I'm not after a partner or a surrogate father for the baby—it was just one stupid kiss and I regret it, because I really did like having you as a friend and I hate that it's been spoilt.'

'You were the one who told me not to drop round,' he pointed out.

'You were glad that I did,' she accused.

She was so honest, all he could do was smile at her again. 'We should have spoken about it,' Ben admitted. 'Tried to work it out.'

'That's what friends do,' Celeste said.

'That's what we are doing,' Ben replied. 'So I guess that's what we are.'

'Honestly?'

'Honestly,' Ben said, and to prove it he squeezed her fat sausage-like fingers. 'Have you got a name for her yet?'

'Nope,' she sighed.

'Any ideas?'

'About a thousand…'

'I'd better get down to work.' He stood up. He wasn't making excuses, he was already five minutes late. 'I'll drop by soon, but call if you need anything.'

'I will.' She gave him a watery smile, glad they were friends again, and so grateful to him for his skill today and for his honesty tonight.

Yet she had been honest too. She didn't want a father for the baby, neither was there a need for a relationship to survive….

And that thought was confirmed when at midnight she finally got to hold her.

She held this little scrap of a thing to her heart and thought it might burst as finally love whooshed in.

She stared at her daughter.

Just a few hours old and so, so , so raw and vulnerable and so reliant on her. No, she didn't need a surrogate father or a partner to make things work for her baby. She would take care of that all by herself.

She just wanted Ben for himself.

'We've been waiting for them.' The midwife cuddled her a little while later when she was wheeled back to bed and the tears finally flooded in. 'You have a good cry…' So she did, soothed that apparently it was completely normal to weep, to sob, that it was obviously hormones on top of an early delivery, estranged parents and a very new, sick little lady who was lying in a cot in Special Care, with a father who didn't care a jot…

Trying to convince herself that her tears had nothing to do with Ben.

* * *

'How is she?'

Ben had washed his hands and put on a gown over his clothes, even though he would only be looking.

'Good.' The special care nurse looked up. 'I'm Bron.'

'Ben.'

'You're the doctor who delivered her?'

'Yep.' Ben peered into the crib. 'I'm a friend of her mum's as well.'

'Well, she had a good first night—she's a restless little thing, aren't you, Willow?'

'Willow?' Ben smiled, because it was the perfect name for her.

She looked so much better than yesterday. Tubes and machines didn't scare Ben. If anything, they reassured him. She was a lovely pinky-red now, and pushing up against the side of the incubator as if she was trying to dig a little hole to climb into.

'I'm just going to change her sheet—do you want to hold her up?'

It would have been appropriate for Ben to help, rather than just stand and watch—and the most natural thing would surely be to just hold her up as the nurse changed the bedding, except, feeling awkward, he declined. 'No, thanks…' He knew he looked arrogant, but it was a price he was willing to pay, so instead he just stood there and watched as the special care nurse changed the bedding, then wrapped bunny rugs into an oval and wrapped them like a little cocoon to help Willow settle. She was a scrap of a thing really, all spindly arms and legs and with a little pink hat covering her dark hair.

She was cute, but no cuter than any of the others he'd

seen as he'd made his way over to her. They could have taken him to any baby and told him that it was Willow and he wouldn't have known any different.

And then she opened her eyes.

Even though she couldn't possibly be doing it, he felt as if she was staring right at him, just as she had in the ambulance. He stared back at her for a moment, and then once again it was he who looked away first.

'Thanks...' He gave a brief smile to the nurse. 'Thanks for letting me see her. It's good to know she's doing well.'

CHAPTER EIGHT

BEN dropped in on Celeste while she was still a patient and occasionally he saw her in the canteen and stopped for a chat and got an update as to how well Willow was doing.

She was doing *so* well.

Every day Celeste saw progress.

And not just with Willow. The ice was thawing with her mother too. She made the journey every other day, initially to see her granddaughter, but bringing in vital supplies for Celeste, then not so vital supplies and sometimes the occasional treat.

It was also Rita who provided an unlikely source of comfort as her milk supply steadily dwindled.

'The more you stress about it, the worse it will be,' Rita said firmly as Celeste sat in tears on the breast pump she hated so much, but at three weeks of age, Willow was only taking the tiniest of feeds from her mother before she became exhausted, and had to be gavage fed through a little tube that ran from her mouth to her stomach. Celeste was struggling to produce enough milk and hated the bland room where she would sit for ages, only to produce a paltry couple of millilitres.

'It's important that she gets my milk.' Celeste gritted her teeth. The lactation consultant had said so.

'It's more important that she gets fed.' Rita refused to back down—she was tired of the pressures that were being placed on her daughter and frustrated on her behalf. 'I couldn't feed you either, Celeste. I had to put you on the bottle when you were four days old.'

'And look how I turned out.'

The weight had fallen off her, sitting there, often teary, jangling with nerves, huge black rings under her eyes thanks to endless two-hourly feeds, broke and a single mum to boot. It was actually her first vague attempt at a joke with her mother in ages and for a moment Rita didn't get it. Then, as she opened her mouth to carry on with her lecture, she did, catching her daughter's eyes and starting to giggle, as did Celeste.

'You turned out just fine,' Rita said when the giggles had faded and the tears that were never very far away these days filled Celeste's eyes. It was the nicest thing her mother had said to her in a very long time. 'Go and get some lunch.' Her mum took the feeble offerings of milk, stuck one of Willow's ID labels on the bottle and popped it in the fridge. 'I'll finish up in here. You go and have a little break.'

Except it didn't feel like a break.

Celeste far preferred the safe routine she had established. Living in the small mothers' area, she was happy with her spartan room and evenings spent chatting with other anxious mothers. Her days were filled with feeding Willow or expressing her milk, gaining confidence with Willow under the nurse's watchful eye and taking for ever to choose what to order from the parents' menu cards that came round once a day. Only every now and then her mother insisted that she 'take a break'. And Celeste loathed it.

There really wasn't much to do.

The hospital *gardens* were a misnomer, the gift shop had long since sold out of her favourite toffees and she'd read each and every magazine at least twice. She'd popped into Emergency a couple of times, but it had always been at the wrong time, the department full and busy, and she'd sat awkward and alone in the staffroom. But mostly she loathed the canteen, where the best way she could describe herself was an 'almost but not quite'.

Almost a member of staff.

Almost a patient.

Almost a mother.

Except she had no uniform.

No ID tag on her wrist.

And no baby beside her.

Worse, her colleagues, if they were there, waved her over and after a couple of moments updating them on Willow's progress, Celeste sat toying with her yoghurt, listening as Deb raved about the wild weekend she'd had and Meg moaned at length about her stint on nights that was coming up.

And then she saw him.

Pushing his tray along as he chose his lunch, Belinda was by his side, dressed in a tight black skirt and red stilettos, her raven curls tumbling down her back as she laughed at something he was saying, and Celeste felt something twist inside her.

Belinda was so ravishing, so sexy and confident and clever and just…so much better suited to Ben.

She was quite sure that if they weren't already together, it was only a matter of time.

'Celeste!' So deep in thought was she that Celeste hadn't even noticed that her colleagues were clearing up the table. 'Did you hear us?' Meg laughed at her absent-mindedness. 'We've got to get back—you drop in any time.'

'I will.'

'And I'm sure you're not thinking of it yet, but when you feel ready, you come and talk to me. Try not to let too much time pass without coming back…'

'I won't.' She said her goodbyes and sat alone, glad of the break. Belinda and Ben wouldn't come over. Registrars didn't generally sit with the nurses, well, in the staffroom they did, of course, but not in the canteen. Meg had unsettled her—of course it was way too soon to be contemplating returning to work, but in a couple of months' time, that was exactly what she would be doing—it was just impossible to comprehend from this vantage point.

'How are you?' Celeste was slightly taken aback by the warmth in Belinda's voice, and even more surprised when she put down her tray and joined her. 'How's Willow?'

'Marvellous.' Celeste blushed slightly as both Belinda and Ben joined her.

'Do you have any idea when you'll get her home?' Belinda pushed.

'A week or two,' Celeste said, 'if she keeps on doing well.' But she'd lost her audience, Belinda excusing herself to answer her pager and suddenly it was just Celeste and Ben.

'You'll be starting to pack up.' Celeste dragged her mind to something that wasn't about Willow. 'It's just a few weeks till you move into your new house now.'

'Actually, it's this weekend,' Ben said. 'The vendor was more than keen for a quick settlement and I'm all ready to move in.'

'Oh.' She was stirring an empty pot of yoghurt. 'I was going to come home for a few hours on Sunday—the nurses are insisting I take a night off. I was going to pop over and say thank you properly…'

'I won't be there,' Ben said, and then there was a pause. 'Of course, I'm only down the road.' Except it wasn't the same.

They were friends, but mainly by proximity, and though she didn't want to rely on Ben, on anyone really, there had been a certain comfort to be had knowing he was just a few doors down.

'Have you got my phone number?' Ben asked. Celeste shook her head and he scribbled it down. 'Here it is.' Ben handed her a card. 'You call if you need anything.'

'Thanks.' She pocketed it as Belinda returned, but they both knew she wouldn't use it. Oh, they'd stop and chat perhaps if she was walking on the beach, but there would be no dropping round, no dinners in front of the television. Just as he was moving so too had she—she was a mother now, which, by his own admission, rendered her off limits to Ben.

Belinda said something that made him laugh and then they tried to include her in the conversation, but it didn't work. She hadn't read a newspaper in weeks, so she wasn't exactly up on current events, hadn't been anywhere except the special care unit, which meant she hadn't a clue about the new seafood restaurant Belinda was raving about. She was just so out of the loop that it was like watching a foreign film. Celeste was so busy reading the subtitles, she missed out on the humour and laughed too late, and by the time she'd worked out what was being said, they had already moved on.

'I'd better get back…' She was about to add 'to feed Willow,' but it was a detail they didn't need. The entire focus of her life was just a conversation filler to them. 'Good luck with the move.'

'Thanks.'

It was a relief to move.

To be away from her—even if it was just down the road—made him safe. There could be no dropping over, no hearing the baby cry as he walked past the unit.

Celeste got under his skin.

From the very first moment he had seen her on the beach she had entranced him—and every now and then, when she was around, somehow he forgot his rules.

But closing the door on the unit for the last time, there was a pang of something—a wave of homesickness almost for the weeks he had spent there, despite the argumentative neighbours and the lack of air-conditioning. It hadn't all been bad, Ben thought as he picked up his sunflowers, which now were up to his shoulders in height, and loaded them in the back of the hire truck, along with the rest of his belongings.

It had almost passed as home.

'I'm sorry to trouble you…' Ben was instantly awake, but as it was only his first night in his new home he struggled to find the light. He could hear the panic in her voice and it had him searching for his jeans the second it was on. 'My car won't start, and I can't get a taxi for an hour…'

'Wait outside,' Ben instructed, not asking what the problem was, because clearly there was one—Celeste would never ring at two a.m. otherwise. 'I'm on my way.'

Used to dressing for an emergency dash to the hospital, he was in jeans, T-shirt and running shoes in less than a minute. Another two had his car out of the garage and down the street, and she was there outside the units, waiting for him.

She'd got so thin. Even in these last few days the weight had fallen off her and she was as white as a sheet in the glare of his headlights. He pulled open the car door and she jumped straight in.

'Thank you. You'll be sorry you gave me your phone number,' she gasped.

'I'm not sorry at all—I'm glad you rang.' He could hear that she was trying not to cry, trying to stay calm, and he didn't push her with questions, just drove and let her speak and tell him the bits she wanted to.

'The car wouldn't start,' Celeste explained. 'I think it's the battery.'

'Don't worry about that now.'

'They said that she's had a couple of apnoea attacks…they haven't happened in a while.'

'Okay…' He forgot to indicate at the roundabout and cursed himself for his error as a car angrily tooted—hell, he did this drive most nights when the hospital called him in. He *had* to concentrate.

'Her temperature's high as well, so they're doing bloods…' He didn't answer, just stared at the road as she talked nervously. 'I told them to ring…' She gulped and then managed to continue. 'I mean, I told them that they were to ring me for anything. So maybe it's not that serious…'

He doubted it.

Despite trying not to worry about Celeste, Ben was. He'd seen her toying with her yoghurt, seen her dramatic weight loss, her nervousness—and she'd practically told him that the nursing staff had insisted she have a night off, so they wouldn't be calling her in the middle of the night for nothing.

'She was doing so well!' Celeste insisted, even though he wasn't arguing. 'I wouldn't have left her otherwise.' God, when did the fear stop? Celeste asked herself. When did you stop living in constant worry?

Get past the first trimester.

Get past thirty weeks.

Get her blood pressure down.

Get past a hellish labour.

Get past those first terrible few nights in Special Care.

Her leg was bouncing up and down, jiggling away.

When did it stop? When did she get to live without fear?

They were at the hospital and he could have just

dropped her off, only of course he didn't, so they parked in the emergency doctor spot and he used his swipe card to get them in the back way, without having to go through Emergency.

'How is she?' Celeste was shaking so much as she went through the hand-washing ritual. The unit was brightly lit even at night, but some of cots were covered in blankets to simulate night.

Not Willow's.

She seemed to have more tubes and people around her than she had on the night after her birth and Celeste was glad when the charge nurse came straight over and brought her up to date.

'She's stable, Celeste.' Her voice was kind and firm and Ben's arm around Celeste helped, just this quiet strength beside her as she took in the news. 'Willow gave us some cause for concern a couple of hours ago—she had an apnoeic episode, which isn't unusual here, but she hasn't had one for a while, then she had another, and she started to struggle a bit with her breathing. Now she'd had some blood gases and we've put her back on CPAP, and the neonatologist has taken blood cultures...'

'Has she got an infection?'

'There are some patchy areas on her X-ray,' the charge nurse replied, 'so we've started her on antibiotics.' They were walking over to her cot and Celeste felt her heart tighten when she saw Willow, seemingly back where she'd started, all wired and hooked up and struggling so hard to breathe.

All Ben wanted to do was turn and run, but instead he stood with his arm around Celeste and stared at the machines instead of the baby. At every turn he was pulled in closer, dragged further into a world where he didn't want to belong.

'She's been fine…' Celeste sobbed when she saw her, the only relief being that Bron, her favourite nurse, was the one looking after her. 'She was going to be moved to the nursery next week…'

'It's just a setback,' the charge nurse said firmly. 'Remember when you first came to the unit and we explained that these little one have ups and downs. Well, Willow has done exceptionally well…' On she went about roller-coaster rides and all the rest of the spiel that Celeste was sick of hearing and had dared to think might be over now. All she felt was that she was back at the start again, especially when she was told she couldn't pick Willow up.

'Just hold her hand for now,' Bron said. 'We're trying to keep her quiet.'

And with that she had to make do.

'Here's Heath coming now. You've met him,' Bron said.

'He's not her doctor,' Celeste pointed out.

'No, he's the consultant on call tonight. Have a seat in the parents room and I'll get him to come and speak with you.'

'Are you the father?' Heath asked Ben as he came up to them.

'No, just a friend,' Ben explained. Then they could see Heath wasn't listening to him as the charge nurse was urgently summoning him back to the cots again.

Celeste could only feel guilty relief that it wasn't for

Willow but for the little one in the next cot. 'Not *just* a friend.' Celeste looked at him. 'There's no such thing as *just* with you.'

Ben tried not to over-analyse that comment too much. It was just one of those things—she was grateful probably that he'd been there tonight, for his help these past weeks, and no doubt glad she didn't have to sit alone on this hellish night, because it wasn't actually Celeste who'd drawn the short straw.

The wait to speak with Heath was endless, and she couldn't go to Willow because, as well as working on her, they were working intensely on the tiny infant in the next cot. Ben thought his job was agony at times, but when the other baby's parents arrived, pale and shocked and visibly terrified, he wouldn't have been Heath or the charge nurse for a million dollars. Unlike Celeste, they got to hold their baby straight away.

Because it was already too late.

'We're concerned about Celeste,' Heath said.

Ben had sat with Celeste until Heath had taken them through Willow's X-rays and blood results and asked all the questions that Celeste was just too overwhelmed to ask, but would surely regret not asking later. Until finally she was taken in to sit with Willow.

'I'm not Willow's father,' Ben interrupted.

'Her partner?'

'No.' Ben shook his head.

'I'm sorry.' Heath frowned. 'Only Bron said that you'd been in a few times at night to see Willow.'

For the first time in his adult life Ben was coming

close to blushing—he felt as if he'd been caught out doing something wrong. Oh, he'd only been up a handful of times—and never when Celeste was around. He'd just wanted to see for himself how the baby was doing.

Clearly, it had been noted!

'I'm a doctor here.' Ben cleared his throat uncomfortably. 'And as I said, Celeste's a friend. I pop in occasionally to check on the baby. I delivered her…'

'I see.' But obviously he didn't.

'You said you were concerned about her?' Ben pursued.

'Look, I thought you were her partner. I'm sorry, my mistake—it's been a long night,' Heath said.

Ben realised that if he wanted to, he could just walk away now—ignore the slight indiscretion, say goodnight to Celeste and just fall into bed for what remained of the night. But he didn't want to.

'We're very good friends,' Ben said. 'If I can help in any way…'

'She just needs a break. It's exceptionally unfortunate that Willow got sick on the one night we'd persuaded her to go home. And with the baby dying in the next cot she's hyper-vigilant now,' Heath explained. 'It's common with mothers in her situation, but sadly tonight has done nothing to help with that.'

'What can I do?' Ben asked.

'It's not simply an overnight thing,' Heath said, standing up and shaking Ben's hand before heading back out to the unit. 'She needs regular support, needs to be encouraged to take a break every now and then— once Willow's better, of course.'

Which meant getting further involved with mother and

child—which Ben definitely didn't want to do. So instead he offered her more practicality as he said goodnight to Celeste. 'Give me your keys. I'll sort out the car for you.'

'I'll sort it out myself tomorrow,' she said.

'Celeste.' He wasn't arguing or debating the point. 'You *need* your car to work, for Willow's sake. So give me your keys, and if it's the battery I'll charge it or get a new one, and if it's something else…' He saw her eyes close in utter despair, as the water rose ever higher. He wanted to pull her out, to wrench her from the rising tide, except he was so very scared to.

Scared to love her.

Except somehow he already did.

Only the problem wasn't Celeste.

It was Willow.

CHAPTER NINE

HE WAS up at six, on a rare day off. He had boxes to unpack and a kitchen to paint, but instead he wandered down the road, Celeste's car keys in hand. He'd have a look at the car, have a run on the beach and then he'd sort out the boxes. Ben opened the garage and after turning the key in the ignition the car grumbled into noisy life—so it wasn't the battery.

At eight he called the mobile mechanic.

'Do you want my advice?' The mechanic stared at what could loosely be called an engine and frowned heavily.

'No.' Ben gave a grimace. 'Just fix it, get it roadworthy, please.'

'The tyres are bald…'

'Get decent second-hand ones,' Ben said, because against that pile of scrap, four gleaming new ones would stand out far too much.

It took the whole day, but by six he was dropping her keys back at the hospital for her.

'How's Willow doing?' he asked her.

'A bit better, thanks.' Celeste looked completely wiped out. Her hair needed washing and there were huge charcoal smudges beneath her eyes, as if she'd been wearing black eyeliner and rubbed them, except she hadn't worn make-up for weeks. 'The first of her blood cultures should be back soon, but she hasn't had a temperature since lunchtime.'

'What about her blood gases?' he queried.

'They're better.' She shook her head in confusion. She wasn't thinking as a nurse but as a mum, listening to the doctors and the special care staff. 'She's to stay on oxygen…'

He wanted more information, wanted to speak with the neonatologist, to see the baby's X-rays and blood results for himself.

'I got to hold her,' she told him tremulously.

His demands had no place here, so instead he smiled. 'That's good news.'

'Mum's in with her now.'

All he could do was take her to the canteen and buy her a hot chocolate and some cereal from the machine, and only when he handed her the car keys did Celeste remember what he was doing here. He wasn't actually here to find out about Willow at all.

'What was wrong with it?' she wanted to know.

'It needed a new battery.' And a starter motor and brake discs and pads and muffler and… But he chose not to elaborate any further.

'How much was it? There's a cash machine here,' she said.

'It wasn't much. We'll sort it out when Willow's better,' Ben said easily. With a baby that sick, Celeste needed a car that started first time every time, Ben told himself. And he was saving his sanity too, he decided. At least he wouldn't be getting woken up at two a.m. any more…

Except he actually hadn't minded.

If the truth be known, he would have hated to have found out from someone else the next day what had happened.

He'd hardly slept in twenty-four hours but, despite that fact, his mind suddenly seemed clear.

Celeste needed a friend—a real one—and maybe he could be that for while, maybe he could be there for her, at least till Willow came home.

'I've been thinking,' Ben said. 'Once Willow's better, how about a day out?'

'Where?' she asked.

'On the water,' Ben suggested, but she immediately shook her head.

'What if something happened? It would take too long to get here,' she protested anxiously.

'We're not crossing the equator, just taking a ride out on the bay! We could have lunch.'

'I don't think so, but thanks anyway.' She shook her head.

'Don't say no,' Ben said. 'Just think about it.'

She didn't think about it.

There was way too much else to think about.

As Willow got over what had turned out to be a nasty bout of pneumonia and started to regularly put on weight, discharge day started looming. Celeste's milk supply had finally completely dried up and, regretfully for Celeste, Willow was now taking a bottle, but at least it did give her a little bit more freedom and meant she could get back to the flat every now and then—or even visit the doctor for herself!

'Celeste?'

Ben passed her as he was walking through the main entrance corridor. Amidst a hub of people and cafés and a gift shop, there was Celeste, as white as a sheet, and in her own vague world.

'Celeste…' He tapped her on the shoulder to get her attention. 'Is everything okay?'

She visibly made an effort to concentrate. 'Fine,' she finally answered.

'Willow?'

'She's good,' Celeste said without the usual elaboration of the past few weeks. Normally she gushed over every milestone, and Ben saw her lick dry lips.

'You?'

'I'm bit queasy,' she admitted. 'I was going to get a drink but there's a huge queue.'

'Go and sit down, I'll get you one.' That she didn't argue told Ben she really wasn't feeling well.

Of course there was a queue at the café, but he could be arrogant enough at times and he ignored it, going straight to the front and getting two bottles of water and a bottle of juice—oh, and a muffin.

'Here.' He put his wares on the table and Celeste took a long drink of water.

'How did you get served so quickly? I'd given up.'

'Perk of the job.' Ben winked. 'I got you something to eat…in case you're hungry.'

Celeste screwed up her nose. 'How much do I owe

you?' She scrabbled in her purse for some money, but Ben just shook his head.

'Don't be daft.'

'Add it to my slate!' Celeste said, and then leant forward, rested her head on her arm for a moment and let everything pass by, the noise, the traffic of a busy hospital, the glare of the windows, everything except Ben's concerned voice.

'Should I be taking your pulse or something?' he teased gently to hide his real worry.

'No.'

'You're not very good company today.' He lifted her forehead a little, then saw her grey face and put it back down to rest on her forearm.

'They told me to wait half an hour…' came her muffled voice. 'I should have listened.'

'Should I be sending for a gurney from Emergency?' he asked lightly.

'Please don't!' Slowly she sat up and gave him a weak smile.

'Better now?'

'Better.' She blew out a breath. 'That's twice you've saved me from embarrassing myself.'

'Childbirth is hardly embarrassing,' he pointed out.

'In the middle of the road, with a crowd gathered?'

'Okay.' He grinned. 'So it could have been embarrassing—if I hadn't managed to get you into the relative privacy of what is now my garden! As would fainting outside the hospital gift shop. So what happened to make you feel like this?'

'I just had my postnatal check.'

'Oh.' He was a doctor, so why were his ears going a bit pink? He could walk into the staffroom in Emergency this very minute into a gaggle of nurses who wouldn't halt their discussion with him in the room.

'He suggested that I have a coil inserted, in the unlikely event that I want to resume sexual relations over the next five years!'

She *did* make him laugh—even at awkward things.

'You will want to, eventually,' he said.

'I doubt it!' She took another long drink and then picked at the muffin. 'It seems like a lot of fuss for nothing, to tell you the truth—well, not nothing,' she mused. 'Having had a family fallout, a baby in Special Care…' She broke off the list of her woes—he wouldn't be interested in all that, especially when she came to the part about how Willow's father didn't want to know her. 'Anyway, he also suggested that I lie down for half an hour afterwards.'

'You clearly didn't listen,' he said a little sternly.

'I felt fine.' Celeste shrugged.

'Well, listen next time,' he ordered.

Colour was coming back to her lips now, and to her cheeks. It had been nice to sit and chat but she'd been gone for a while now and wanted to be back to give Willow her bottle.

'I'd better get up to Special Care…'

She was still a touch pale. 'Maybe you should wait another ten minutes,' he suggested.

Which she probably would have, except the pager she wore went off, telling her that Willow was awake and ready to be fed.

'I should go.'

'I'll walk up with you,' Ben offered, still concerned with her colour.

They walked through the corridors and up to the lift, Ben seeing her right up to the entrance to Special Care, and as they arrived, Celeste was suddenly nervous.

'Do you want to come in?' It was, oh, so casually offered. 'You'll see a huge difference in her…'

'I'd love to,' Ben said, and she could hear the 'but' even before it was said, knew it was coming before it was uttered. 'But I really ought to get back to Emergency. Another time, maybe?'

'Sure.' She didn't get him—just didn't. He seemed to enjoy her company, was always there when she needed him, and yet sometimes all he wanted to do was get away from her!

'Hey…' He turned around. 'Have you thought about coming out on the boat with me?'

'I don't think so,' Celeste declined. 'They're saying that Willow might be ready for discharge next Monday, and I've got loads to get ready.'

'Well, I'm off next weekend,' Ben said. 'So the offer's there…just let me know.'

She was ready.

Well, as ready as she would ever be!

All the new baby clothes had been washed in soap flakes, there were nappies and baby wipes and bottles and formula, the crib that Ben had set up and which Celeste had lined with bunny rugs. All it needed now was Willow—and that was happening tomorrow.

The nurses had practically frogmarched her out of the department, insisting she spend a day at home and strongly suggesting she didn't come back till morning—that she should grab one last night of uninterrupted sleep while she still could.

Her parents, having helped her set up, had gone home, and with nothing to do, Celeste had decided to walk down the road to get a magazine, with the intention of sitting on the beach to read it. Or rather that was her excuse for walking past Ben's new house!

It felt strange, being out in the fresh air—strange to be out in the afternoon sunlight instead of in the nursery—but the nurses had given her very little choice in the matter, so she decided to enjoy it.

She was wearing denim shorts and a white halter-neck T-shirt, pre-pregnancy clothes that were actually a bit big for her now. Her feet were wrapped in thin red leather sandals, and it felt nice to have the sun on her legs, nice to walk along the street, though she felt as if she'd forgotten something, kept pulling out her phone to check it in case the hospital had rung and she'd missed it, or kept scrambling in her bag to check she had her keys. It already felt completely weird to be anywhere without Willow.

Still, the world had carried on very nicely without her. Flowers hung heavy on the trees, the bay was blue and still glistening in the background—and there was Ben, with his new boat all hooked up to his four-wheel drive.

'Very nice.' Celeste commented, walking around and inspecting *his* new baby. 'Very nice indeed.'

'I think I'm in love.' Ben grinned, running a loving

hand over his new toy, and all Celeste could do was laugh. 'How's Willow?'

'Very well. She looks like a complete fraud—she's way too healthy to be in hospital.'

'All ready for tomorrow?' he asked.

'As ready as I'll ever be.'

'You'll be great,' he said reassuringly.

'So, are you taking her out?' She wouldn't ask to go with him, Celeste decided, but if he happened to offer again...

'I've just got back,' Ben said. 'I went out with a friend—I'm still not sure about launching her on my own yet.'

'Ooh, no!' Celeste agreed, smiling, but her heart sank a little, realising that she had very literally missed the boat with him. 'The boat ramp is not the place to practise.'

'Yeah, I'm still a novice—but it is nice to be out there again. I'd forgotten how good it feels.'

'There's another launching ramp by the creek,' Celeste said, 'for when you do want to take her out on your own. It's probably the quietest one and you won't be holding everyone up.'

'You've done this before, then?' he asked curiously.

'All the time,' Celeste said with a cheeky grin. 'Well, when Dad and I were talking, I used to go fishing with him.'

'You?' Ben raised his eyebrows. 'Fishing?'

'No, daydreaming,' Celeste said. 'But I'm fishing now...'

It took a second for him to get her meaning and when he did he smiled.

'Let's go, then.'

It was the perfect evening to try out a new boat—the bay was calm, with barely a breeze. For a novice, he did a pretty decent job of reversing the boat and trailer down the ramp, then jumped out and dealt with the boat as Celeste took the driver's seat, just as she had when she had been out with her dad. Having parked his four-wheel drive, she then walked down to the water, Ben holding her hand as she stepped in. His new engine purred into life and she was so glad she had said yes, so glad, as Ben weaved the boat, to feel the wind in her hair and to just breathe again after these last few weeks.

Ben watched as slowly, slowly she unwound.

The weight had fallen off her since Willow's birth, and seeing her slender frame emerging he'd realised just how ill she'd been, probably since the day he'd met her. Too much time in the hospital, both as a patient and visiting Willow, had given her that pale, unhealthy colour. Still, the sea air was bringing back some much-needed warmth to her cheeks and when she didn't check her phone for a full ten minutes, Ben knew that finally, even if it was just for a little while, the Celeste of old was back.

They stopped and idled and Ben set out the food they had grabbed on a quick stop at the deli. In the distance, Melbourne glittered gold in the setting sun. Willow was coming home tomorrow and all was surely right in the world—even if it felt otherwise at times.

'Scared about tomorrow?' Ben asked.

'Scared but ready,' Celeste admitted.

'You're going to be a great mum,' Ben said.

'I'd better be…' Celeste smiled. 'She'll be home in a matter of hours.'

He unpacked tarragon chicken in mayonnaise, which tasted as good as they first time they'd shared it, washed down with sparkling mineral water. For Celeste it was bliss to just pause, to escape before life changed yet again tomorrow.

'You've got transport and everything sorted?' Ben checked.

'Dad and Mum are coming,' Celeste informed him. 'Come over in the afternoon if you like—I've got some friends coming round and we're going to have a little barbeque…'

'Shouldn't you take it easy the first few days?' Ben asked dubiously.

'That's the plan,' Celeste said with a flash of her old cheek. 'I'll get them all in and out in one hit!'

They could have headed home then, except they didn't. Ben was playing sailor while Celeste lay in the bottom of the little boat, her feet up on the edge, and listened to the dreamy lap, lap of the water. She couldn't remember being this relaxed since Willow's birth, since before Willow was born, since for ever, really…

When she opened her eyes to tell him so, she suddenly wasn't relaxed any more.

Because he was watching her, just sitting quietly watching her. When Celeste's eyes opened, he didn't look away, he just stared, and she stared right back at those contrary green eyes that both reached for her and resisted her. They stared in silence, reliving their one and only kiss in their minds, and all it did was confuse her, because in that second she was sure that without Willow there would be love between them.

Without Willow.

It was an impossible place and one she never wanted to visit. She could see a flash in his eyes and it could have been the breeze or the sun glare, or it might have been tears, because there was regret etched on his features, and regret laced with anger in hers.

Because without Willow, they'd be mere colleagues now.

Without Willow she'd never have been living opposite him.

There could be no without Willow and there could be no them.

'Rotten timing, huh?' She wasn't making a joke, and she wasn't making a stab in the dark as to how he was feeling—because out on the water, when it was just the two of them, with no past, no future, just this moment in time, there was no question of either of them denying it.

'It is,' Ben said, and he didn't have to elaborate—he'd stated his case from the very beginning.

'So I'm not going mad and imagining things, then?'

'You're not going mad…' He touched her hair, just holding one heavy curl in his fingers, and *how* he wanted to tell her, to explain, but how? Heath's warning was ringing in his ears. This was her day off from worrying and he didn't want to darken it with his grief, couldn't burden this very new mum with his fears for her, for her child.

'I just can't do it.' Ben settled for that.

'I know.'

'I said so from the beginning.'

'You did.'

'Can we still be friends?' Ben asked, and her answer was the same as the one ringing inside his own head.

'I don't know.'

Maybe this was their last kiss but it was the sweetest she had ever tasted.

He bent her head and brushed her lips and if real men didn't cry, that excluded Ben, because she felt the brush of damp eyelashes on her cheeks as his mouth met hers. It was the most fleeting of kisses but it was so mingled with regret and love that it would stay with her for ever.

She didn't have to tell him to take her home afterwards, he just started up the engine, Ben driving, Celeste pulling on massive sunglasses and trying not to cry.

The whole journey home was neither pleasant nor wretched, yet contained no more kisses.

'Do you want to come in?' she offered when he pulled up at her gates. She knew exactly what she was offering, knew because the air was so thick with want, there could be no doubt in either of their minds.

'Celeste...' His knuckles were white where he gripped the steering-wheel. 'Go inside.'

'Just for tonight,' she pleaded. She wanted a proper kiss goodbye, was greedy for more, and was trying to convince herself she could handle the morning after. Rejection was surely her forte—except she loathed it now.

''Night, Celeste,' he replied.

CHAPTER TEN

HE PROBABLY should have popped over.

Set the tone.

Resumed being nothing but friends.

Only it was too late for that now.

Autumn was coming. Every night the wind stripped a few more petals from the sunflowers. Heading for home from work nearly a week later and sick of the constant reminders, Ben pulled out the gangly stalks and went to shove them on the compost. About a hundred seeds scattered in the garden while he did it and Ben gritted his teeth. So much for forgetting! If he didn't get the seeds up he'd need a scythe next year just to get to the front door!

She was everywhere.

In his head, in his dreams, and as he walked into the house, he headed upstairs to change and his eyes moved straight to the beach, to where he'd first seen Celeste, instead of to the picture of Jen on his bedside table.

'What do I do?' He picked up the silver frame and stared into his wife's clear eyes and wished for just two minutes of her time.

Two minutes of her logical, practical advice, which

was a stupid thing to wish for—as if he should even be asking Jen about Celeste!

He wanted her to tell him, just a sign, one little sign, only he didn't even know what he was asking for.

And then he looked at the whole picture, not just at Jen.

He ran a finger over the swell of her stomach to where their baby lay, touched *her* only through glass, touched what he'd never, not even once got to hold.

But there wasn't time to wallow. He had visitors that evening, which proved difficult, and then he was called into hospital to deal with an emergency at around 10 p.m. He could hear the pounding music from Celeste's neighbours as he drove past her unit and despite his best intentions, it was difficult to ignore. However, he determinedly drove on, hoping the party would wind down early, or that she'd taken Willow and gone to her parents'. Surely a wild party next door was the last thing a new mum needed only a few days after bring her babe home.

Still, it wasn't his problem now.

'Sorry!' Belinda looked up from a packed Resus as Ben made his way over. 'You're about to get a page saying we don't need you after all.'

'Sure about that?' Ben checked, because the place was steaming.

'We were alerted for two multi-traumas,' Belinda explained, 'and on top of this amount of patients, I thought we should call in some extras, even though you're not rostered on.'

'Where are the trauma victims?'

'One died en route and one's not too seriously injured.

I'm just about to ring the parents—who'd have teenagers, huh? Perhaps I should have waited to call you.'

'Better not to wait and see.' Ben really didn't mind being called in, it was part of his job. 'I'll give you a hand now that I'm here.'

'No, you won't,' Belinda contradicted as she looked at some X-rays on the computer. 'Go and get some sleep—this is just a usual Friday night.'

'I really don't mind,' he persisted.

'Well, I do,' Belinda said. 'You're covering for me tomorrow, remember.'

'Ah, yes!'

'And I'm rather hoping that you *won't* be calling me in.' She winked at him.

'Going somewhere nice?' he asked.

'To a fabulous hotel in the City.' Belinda smiled. 'A million miles away from here.'

'You and Paul still going strong, then?'

'Absolutely. You know you really shouldn't knock the internet.'

Ben just groaned—she never let up! 'Okay, then, I'll head home. Just buzz if you do need help, though.'

He would actually have preferred to be working— wished that Belinda had handed him a pile of patient cards and asked him to wade his way through them, because as he turned into his street, instead of slowing down he speeded up a touch and turned up the car radio. Really, whatever was going on at the flats wasn't his problem. There were parties there every other night, and he couldn't forever be checking that Celeste was okay…

A group of teenagers was spilling onto the street, and

despite the car radio on loud he could hear the doof-doof of the music. Though he had driven past, regretting it, resenting it even, he executed a hasty U-turn, flashed his lights at the drunken idiots and pulled over. Opening the gates and heading up to her unit, he saw the lights were on. Hearing Willow's screams from inside, he knocked at the door.

When there was no answer he realised how scared she must be.

'Celeste,' he called during a tiny lull in the music. 'It's me, Ben.'

'What do you want?' He could see she'd been crying when she opened the door.

'I heard the noise on my way back from work. You can't settle her in this. You should have rung me…'

'You wouldn't have been home,' Celeste pointed out, but despite her flip retort he could tell she was still close to tears. 'It's only a party…'

Which it was—a very loud party, but next door to a very new baby and a very new mum, who just hadn't needed it tonight.

'I can't get her to feed, and the nurses said it had to be every three hours at the most,' she said forlornly.

'Come on,' he announced. 'Let's grab her things and you can both crash at my place.'

She was about to say no, about to close the door, but a small fight was erupting in the next unit, and, however much she didn't want to need help, tonight she did.

'Please, Celeste…' Even inside her flat the music was just as loud! 'Pack a bag and come and stay at my house tonight,' he begged again.

She would have argued, but she was too relieved. She wasn't sure if it was her own tension or the noise that was upsetting Willow, but after six weeks of tender care in the special care unit, Celeste was scared enough being on her own with her, without the invasive noise and chaos of next door.

She was trying to clip Willow in her little seat to carry out to the car, but Ben had other ideas. 'Just put her in her pram. It will be just as easy to walk…and she can sleep in it.'

She would never have walked outside with the party mob there, but with Ben she felt safe. He pushed the pram and bumped it down the steps as Celeste locked up. The gates to the units were already open and with his arm around her they walked in swift silence away from the noise along the street and only when it faded in the distance did he talk.

'You should have called the police.'

'What, and have my neighbours hate me?' Celeste said ruefully as they walked along the street. There was a nearly full moon, which provided plenty of light, the music was just a thud in the distance and she could hear the welcome sound of the water now. 'It was only a party…' she said again.

'It's no place…' He didn't finish the sentence, but Celeste knew what he'd been about to say.

'It's all I can afford, Ben,' she told him quietly.

'I know that.'

'There was a small house in town for about the same price—I should have rented that, but I wanted to be closer to the beach. The flat seemed fine when I inspected it. I didn't think to ask to see it at eleven o'clock on a Friday night…' She took over the pram, and was walking more quickly now. Willow, over-tired, was still crying, and Celeste was both annoyed at him and at herself. She was trying so hard to cope, so hard to do right by her baby, yet at every turn she seemed thwarted, at every turn life tossed her another curve ball… 'I'm doing my best,' she said as they arrived at his house. 'Though, I'm sure you don't think it's good enough—'

'I never said that!' Ben interrupted.

'No, but you think it!' she retorted. She was angry at him and she knew she shouldn't be. It wasn't his fault, he was being perfectly nice, but his home, his order, his everything only seemed to highlight her own inadequacies.

'Why don't you feed her?' Ben suggested soothingly. He carried the pram and the baby up the stairs and past his stunning bedroom to a rather nice guest room, where he parked the pram. 'Rest on the bed, the view's lovely. You can both relax and get Willow calm and settled…'

'And her mum too…' She was just a bit embarrassed at her outburst. After all, it wasn't his fault how he made her feel.

'I'll leave you to it,' Ben said. 'I'll find some sheets to make up the bed.'

'Thanks,' she said awkwardly.

'Come out when you're ready.'

'I need…' He was turning to go and she stopped him, rummaging through Willow's bag. 'Is there anywhere I can warm up her bottle?'

'Sure,' he said.

'Actually…' she picked up the hot little bundle that was her sobbing baby '…could you hold Willow for me?'

'I'll do the bottle,' Ben said, in an annoyingly calm voice that only made her appear more frazzled. 'I know where everything is.'

He took the bottle and she changed Willow while her screams quadrupled. She felt like howling herself. She knew he'd been expecting her to just lie on the bed and flop out a boob, to feed her baby herself…

She felt such a failure, felt so close to crying that she barely managed to thank him as he returned a couple of moments later with a warm bottle. He sort of hovered for an uncomfortable moment as she sat awkwardly on the edge of the bed and took it from him. Then Willow's mouth clamped onto the teat as if she'd been starved for a week and the only sound was of gulps and tears as an overtired baby finally took its bottle from an over-wrought mum.

Although Willow was gulping her bottle, she kept jumping and startling while she was doing it. Celeste kicked off her sandals and lay back on the bed, pulling Willow in tighter, but every time she almost relaxed, the baby would suddenly startle as if the noise, the angst, the panic from her mother was all about to start again.

It was nothing unfamiliar to Celeste.

The party had just been the clincher. In the few days since she'd been home from the hospital, practically every time she'd sat down to quietly feed her babe, her mother had 'dropped in', offering all kinds of sugges-tions—'Change her first,' or 'Change her after she's fed,' or 'Hold the bottle higher,' or 'She needs winding,' each well-meaning suggestion from Rita only exacerbating the tension further.

Celeste desperately wanted to be back in the hospital, wanted to be feeding Willow with knowledgeable staff offering quiet encouragement, or even to put her to bed in the hospital at night and go home, as she had last Sunday, missing her but knowing she was being well looked after—no, that Willow was being *better* looked after than she could manage by herself.

'It's okay, Willow, it's all okay, Willow,' she said softly, over and over again until finally Willow believed it, until finally her little jerks and startles stopped, and the gulps of tears faded. Celeste felt this unfamiliar surge of triumph as her baby relaxed into her, scared to move almost as Willow moved from resisting her to this passive, trance-like state almost—seemingly asleep, but still feeding.

She really was asleep, Celeste realised as she took the empty bottle from Willow's mouth and watched her little eyelids flicker.

So asleep that if the party down the street relocated to outside the bedroom window, Celeste was quite sure that Willow wouldn't wake up.

And she had done it all by herself.

She'd never been so alone with her baby and felt so much a mum at the same time.

Celeste stared down at the perfect features of her daughter, dark little eyebrows that looked as if they'd been pencilled on, her fine pointy nose and little rosebud mouth, and she thought her heart would swell and burst there was so much love inside it for her baby.

A scary love that knew no bounds—yet still she felt so inadequate.

This little scrap of a thing was just so utterly and completely dependent on her, there should be no room to feel anything else.

Except she did.

She didn't want to move, didn't want to put her down. She just wanted to stay safe on this bed, holding her baby, watching the bay with Ben just a call away. To simply hold onto this first ray of peace.

'Don't fall asleep holding the baby.'

She could hear her mother as if she were in the room with them.

And she was right, Celeste sighed, heading over to the pram and gently lowering Willow in.

As she headed out to the lounge, Ben, sprawled on one of the sofas, looked up from the show on the television he was watching and poured her a glass of wine. It was the second little ray of peace she felt. For the first time since Willow's discharge from hospital, she felt as if she were home.

'She's asleep,' she told him.

'Good. How are you?' he asked.

'Better.' She took a seat on the edge of the sofa opposite him. 'You always seem to bailing me out. It won't be for much longer.'

'I know,' Ben said, then suggested that she choose a movie, so she did, kneeling down as she worked through his collection, and as she did she told him her most recent news.

'I mean, you won't have to keep bailing me out because I'm moving back home.'

His wine paused midway to his mouth. 'When?' he asked and then took a long sip, holding it in his mouth until she replied.

'Next weekend.' Huge amber eyes flashed towards him then looked away. 'Mum and Dad are painting the spare room for her and we're moving the stuff through-out next week. It's just not working, living here. You know what it's like, and Mum and I are getting on a lot better now…' She trailed off.

'How do you feel about it?' he asked shrewdly.

Celeste stared unseeingly at the DVD she was holding. 'To be honest, I haven't really stopped to think about it that much.'

So she did. She sank back on her heels and thought.

Out loud.

'It's not what I really want,' she admitted. 'I asked them a few weeks ago, but that was when I was preg-nant. I never wanted to live there with a baby—but it's best for Willow. We could manage on our own, but this way…' Celeste took a deep breath. 'She's nearly two months old—it seems unbelievable. I could put her in the crèche next month and start back at work.'

'Is your mum going to watch her for you?'

Celeste nodded. 'Only for work—she's warned me that she's not a built-in babysitter so we've agreed it's just for a year.' And then she told him her other news. 'I've spoken to Meg and she's going to help me with my application to transfer hospitals.'

'Back to your old one?'

'No.' Instantly she shook her head. 'To Melbourne Central…'

'That's my old stomping ground,' Ben said.

'It's much closer to home than here. Anyway, I'm going to be head down finishing the emergency grad year and then I'm going to do as many shifts as I can and save…'

She looked so young sometimes—she *was* so young, Ben reminded himself. Only that wasn't what he meant. She seemed so fey and carefree at times yet there was a deep streak to her that enthralled him—an inherent resilience that belied her apparent fragility at times.

And she'd clearly given this a lot of thought.

'You say you're getting on with your parents now?'

'It's a lot better than it was.' She'd chosen the movie and popped it in. 'I can't imagine living at home again, though. I couldn't wait to leave the first time!' She rolled her eyes and added, 'They're really strict.' She gave him a smile and this time sat on the same sofa as him. 'There'll be none of this…'

'What?'

'Sitting in the dark with a man, drinking wine!'

'You're twenty-four.' Ben grinned. 'And we're watching a movie.'

'I don't care how old you are, young lady.' She wagged a finger at him. 'When you're under our roof, you live by our rules.'

'You're serious?' he exclaimed, half horrified, half amused.

'Absolutely. It will be even worse this time around, given…' She nodded in the direction of upstairs.

'She can't hear you!' Ben laughed.

'I don't care whether she can hear or not. I've told Mum and Dad that there's to be no talk of "the mess I've got myself into" or "accidents" around her—that's *my* only rule if I move home. I'll put up with anything for a year if it gives her a better start, but I'll tell her her story in my own way, in my own time.'

'That's fair enough.'

'It's not her fault I didn't know her dad was married…' She stopped talking then, thankful for the dark room, because her face was red suddenly, not from embarrassment but near tears. They sat in silence for a while—the words that had never been voiced by Ben hanging there between them…

'How, Celeste?' he finally asked. 'How did you not know?'

'I just didn't.'

'What about nights like this?'

'Like what?'

'Like this.' Ben gestured at the simplicity of it all. 'Did you never wonder why it was always at yours?'

'He didn't come to mine.' Her voice was shrill. 'We went out, we were dating…'

He didn't get it, but it wasn't his place to push it, he'd already crossed that line, so Ben chose to leave it, surprised when it was Celeste who broke the strained silence between them.

'I shared with two other students. I knew what we were doing was wrong…' She stopped again and was staring unseeingly at the television screen.

'Wrong?' Ben frowned. 'I thought you didn't know he was married?'

'It's more than that. I can't tell anyone about Willow's father…it would cause so much trouble.'

'You can tell me,' Ben said, because though he could sense her indecision, he also sensed her burden.

'You won't say anything to anyone?'

'Never.'

'Because gossip…'

'I don't gossip.'

She looked over to him, at those guarded, remote features that occasionally softened into tenderness—and right now she was the lucky recipient of that emotion. She saw the honesty and integrity there too and it made her shame burn harder, so much so that she couldn't look him in the eyes as she shared her truth.

'His name's Dean. He was my lecturer at university.' When Ben didn't say anything, she wasn't sure if he understood the problem. 'It's forbidden for a lecturer to have a relationship with a student…'

'I know.'

'It happens, though,' she attempted to rationalise. 'All the time. I mean, it's between two consenting adults, and it's a stupid rule really…' He could see tears squeezing out of her eyes, and, as she always did, she closed them, trying to keep it all in.

'Not that stupid a rule, perhaps,' Celeste admitted. 'He must choose his targets—I mean, he had his story all set up. He said he shared a house with another lecturer—that was why we couldn't go back there—and as I was sharing with students, we always went out miles away. Of course, I assumed it was so that no one from uni found out about us. He told me that once I'd qualified, that we could go more public...'

'You never suspected?' He still didn't get it. Even if he and Celeste were only a little bit in each other's lives, that much of each other they already knew.

'I'd never really had a serious boyfriend,' she revealed, giving a tight shrug. 'Like I said, Mum and Dad were really strict, and when I left home, I didn't go wild or anything. Really, I didn't even know if we were going out at first, it was just a drink, or dinner...' She was squirming with embarrassment now. 'And we went to a hotel a couple of times...it should have been obvious to me,' Celeste admitted. 'I mean, he never answered his phone—it always went to voicemail.'

'Oh?' Ben frowned. 'Is that supposed to mean something?'

'He never answered his phone when he was with me either.'

'Okay...' Ben said, not that he really understood it.

'You're too honest.' Celeste managed a watery smile. 'So am I, I guess, because I never assumed he was lying. He never answered his phone in case it was another of his women—or even his wife.'

'How *did* you find out he was married?'

'He was away one day, another lecturer came in— explaining that he was taking over because apparently Dean's wife was ill...'

'Oh, Celeste,' Ben groaned softly.

The commercials for the film were over so she put her feet up on the table because that was what Ben was doing and took a sip of her wine and sat there, trying to watch the film while remembering the hurt—the very real hurt—and the fear a few weeks later when she'd found out that she was having Dean's baby.

It was a funny movie that she'd chosen, or it had been the first time she'd watched it—only it didn't seem so funny now. Instead, it was a romantic comedy of errors that just made her feel like crying.

Ben was on the sofa next to her, big and solid and so reassuring.

And there was a picture of Jen by the television.

She couldn't see the image, just the outline of the frame—but that made her feel like crying too.

As if the universe had got something terribly wrong, had tossed them all up in the air and they'd landed in the wrong places, the wrong rooms, with the wrong people.

Except she liked being here with him.

She needed a tissue, Celeste realised, had sniffed four times in the past fifteen seconds and it was getting embarrassing now, except she had to reach over him to get them, so she didn't bother. 'Here.' He pulled a wad out of a box on the coffee table and Celeste managed a wry laugh.

'Do you sit here crying at films often?'

'Nope…' Ben smiled at the image she conjured up. 'Jen's sister was over earlier.'

Oh, God!

She didn't say it, but she flinched at her insensitivity. Wallowing in her own problems, he just seemed so together, it was so easy to forget all he'd been through. 'Just for a quick hi, but she hadn't seen the house.'

'It must have been hard for you,' she said.

'Yes, it was,' Ben admitted. 'Thankfully I was called into work.'

'Thank you.' She stared over to him. 'I mean, really, thank you for everything.'

'I was glad to help.'

'And I'm sorry.'

'For what?' Ben asked, but was just a touch uncomfortable as to how she might answer.

'Because of how difficult things are between us…'

'They're not difficult,' he lied.

'Yes, they are,' Celeste contradicted, 'because I *want* to be friends with you, Ben, but I don't know how to *be* one…' He could see the tears rolling down her cheeks now. 'And please don't feel guilty when I tell you this, but it's part of the reason I'm moving home too—maybe things will be easier, maybe we might even manage to be *friends*.'

'I don't think so.' His fingers wanted to touch her hair again, he wanted to hold her, to kiss her, but it would be too cruel to them both.

But then she looked at him, looked right at him, and said the words that sometimes he'd wished too, stuck her toe in that closing door and kept it wedged that little bit open.

'I wish it could have been you. I wish Willow was yours.'

She meant it, she really meant it, and her nose was running because she meant it so much.

She wished it had been Ben, that he had been the one who'd made love to her.

Wished, wished, wished for so much more than the little they'd had.

'It would never have been me,' Ben said then. 'Because I'd have taken so, so much more care of you than he did.'

He couldn't stand that she was moving away, couldn't stand the thought of not seeing her again, couldn't stand not to touch her some more. 'Come here.' He pulled her at her wrist so she was right up against him and it was like climbing into his boat.

Sort of away from everything.

It was nice to have a cuddle with him while she cried—he was so big she *had* to lean against him, or she'd topple overboard! Nice when he hooked his arm around her and secured her there.

Just really, really nice.

It was for Ben too.

So rarely was he indulgent—but next week she was going somewhere she didn't really want to go.

Leaving him somewhere he didn't really want to be.

Tonight they were here.

And it was nice.

Nice to lie on the sofa with *her.*

Nice to hear her sobs recede and to feel her chest move as she laughed at the film.

It had been a hell of a day. Showing Abby and her husband Mick around the house, with Abby tearing up every five minutes, he'd even offered to take them out on the boat.

Except Abby looked too much like Jen and there would be three in the boat instead of four—so he'd been glad when he'd been called in to work.

It had just been one of those days, and it could have been one of those nights too.

Except Celeste was here and all it felt was right.

He was hovering on the edge of indecision, scared but almost ready to really make a new start.

A very new start.

Certain films shouldn't be watched with a supposed friend who was actually a whole lot more.

They were watching a passionate on-screen kiss— and it seemed to go on a lot longer than Celeste remembered from the last time she had seen the film.

It was like the time when at fourteen she'd been watching a serious documentary with her parents and suddenly they had been watching full-on sex.

Just exquisitely uncomfortable—but for all sorts of different reasons tonight.

His hand was hovering over her stomach, but she was too near the edge of the sofa, needed a little shift, a little hoist from him to bring her closer, which he didn't do, so Celeste wriggled back a bit.

Just a bit.

Ever the gentleman, he moved back a fraction and secured her, his hand on her stomach, and she felt like pulling up her knees, because she'd felt him touch her.

She couldn't remember how to breathe, because there was this feather-light stroking from his fingers on her stomach, just these almost indistinguishable caresses and a slight irregularity to his breathing as they continued to watch the kissing on the screen.

'When you move home….' His voice was hesitant, slightly gruff. 'Suppose we take things slowly…' She could hardly breathe, hardly dared to hope, scared to move in case he stopped talking. 'Suppose we go out…?'

'I won't have a babysitter—Mum only said she'd do it while I worked,' she whispered back.

'You could come here, we could have dinner, just start at the very beginning, get to know each other properly…'

'And Willow?' Her heart was in her mouth.

'If we take it slowly enough, maybe…' He could hear the blood pounding in his ears as he offered so much more than he had sworn he ever would. 'Maybe in time…'

He was offering her hope—offering *them* hope—that the impossible might just happen.

CHAPTER ELEVEN

CELESTE suddenly didn't care about the film, she wanted to see him, so she wriggled around and his legs had to trap hers to stop her falling off the sofa. He could see her lovely eyes shining in the darkness and he wanted to protect her, even from herself, but, God, he also wanted to kiss her, to just dive straight into that pleasure, but he had to make it very clear too.

'We'll just take things slowly.'

'I know.'

And then he could kiss her—properly this time—and she could kiss him too, a lovely slow kiss that wasn't awkward, just took a little adjusting to, because she was lower than him and rather precariously balanced, so he pulled her in a bit so that her bare thigh had to be clamped by his denimed ones, and as his tongue slid into her mouth, as their lips pressed harder, if she wanted to stay on the sofa, her other leg had to wrap around his.

He smelt like Ben…like the kiss from the first time, except she felt sexy now rather than tired, she felt alive rather than weary, and she felt wanted rather than looked after.

It made her feel dizzy.

She was sucking on his bottom lip, her little hand on his broad back and with the roughness of his jeans in her groin.

'Celeste…' He pulled back a bit as she pressed hard into him. 'I thought we were taking it slowly!'

'Not with this part,' she murmured.

Like teenagers, with no real intent, they kissed, except, unlike the rest of his body, his arm was going to sleep, so he pulled her onto her back and lay on top of her, his elbows sinking into the sofa as he kissed her deeply.

It *was* a kiss that was safe, because they weren't going anywhere more serious at the moment. At some level they both knew that, but it had to be verbally confirmed.

'We can't,' Ben said as her thigh slid between his legs and her hand slid up the back of his T-shirt, feeling the silk of his skin, the firmness of muscle, and she arched towards him. 'I haven't got anything.'

'I know,' she breathed. 'But I had a coil inserted…'

'No.' He stopped then, because she was just too precious to risk it. 'You're not to rely on just that.'

'So just kissing, then…' Her mouth was on his, her body this writhing mass of want beneath his. It was already more than a kiss but, God, it felt nice.

'I think we can manage a little more than that,' he promised. His hand was creeping up her top now, her breast soft and warm beneath his fingers. This was *so* much more than a kiss as his fingers skilfully caressed her nipples.

She'd considered her breasts useless, shrunken little failures, having not been able to breastfeed Willow, but now they swelled beneath his fingers, and the feel of his mouth and his tongue on them was sublime.

She was pressing into him, could feel his erection, and she wanted it closer…

'Ben…' she murmured softly. She could feel these little licks of pleasure in her stomach and it startled her, for he was turning her on her side, with nowhere to go except the back of the sofa and the gorgeous weight of Ben pinning her. Her hand crept to the front of his jeans; she felt the lovely solid length of him and heard him moan. 'Ben…' She didn't know why she kept saying his name, but she couldn't help it. Her fingers started working the heavy buckle of his belt, but his hand stopped her.

'No, this is just for you,' he said. He didn't mean it in a martyred way, he was lost too, but somewhere inside he wanted her to know that it could be about her, that it could just be about this…

He was kissing her hard, this lovely wet kiss that was so deep she didn't want to move or breathe again.

Was there any place nicer to be than on a sofa with her?

He was eighteen again—only it hadn't been that good then.

He was peeling open the zipper of her shorts, wriggling them down over her bottom. As he pressed her body against his, his mouth was on her neck, kissing her, trying to remember not to leave any marks, because it was the last thing she needed with her mother. He was glad he didn't have a condom in the house because he so badly wanted to dive into her. He was holding her hips now, guiding her along his hard length still safely under his jeans. He thought he might explode from the delicious pressure building, but was determined that he wouldn't—because even now it was still about her.

For Celeste was lost within herself, savouring and catching up on everything she'd ever missed—those little licks of pleasure inside her were building to a crescendo. She could hear humming, and realised it was her; she was humming as she coiled her legs around him, coming just to his kiss, coming just for Ben.

'Willow…' she gasped, feeling as if she'd been drinking as the piercing tone of her baby's cries brought her back down to a rather nice place. His kiss welcomed her back slowly as she worked out that she could, in fact, breathe, and then on wobbly legs and dishevelled she stood there in front of him, hauling her shorts back up her legs, more than a little embarrassed but at the same time not.

Then she gave him that wonderful smile and he smiled back and she decided that even if that embrace was all it could be for now—it was more than enough.

Quite simply it was the nicest thing that had happened to her.

Ben had never expected to feel again.

Over the years he had tried and over the past few weeks he had resisted, but feelings didn't listen to logic.

Finally, he was starting to believe.

There were two glasses on the draining board, her footsteps were on the stairs as she came back down from soothing Willow and there was this delicious presence that filled each room. For the first time in years he was glimpsing a future—not in bricks or gardens, or hours filled with work, but hours and—later on—nights with her.

Maybe he *could* get used to this.

'Hey!' She was standing at the kitchen, hands behind her back, her dark brown hair black in the low living-room light. Her eyes were glittering and she was wearing a provocative smile that demanded caution.

'How's Willow?' he asked.

'Asleep again,' Celeste said. 'How are you?'

'Good,' Ben said, because he was. Having Celeste here was making him feel wonderful.

God, she was gorgeous, standing there just smiling, her cheeks all flushed, eyes glittering, the top button of her shorts undone.

He was hard again so he turned away, made a big show of washing the two glasses, just to give himself time to recover.

She walked over and kissed him on the lips and he kissed her back, his arms wrapping around her, wet, soapy hands holding her, but she didn't hold him back, she just kissed him.

'Which hand?' She pulled her lips away and smiled up at him wickedly.

He frowned. 'What are you up to?'

'Which hand?' she repeated.

He was smiling and frowning simultaneously. He was beginning to get a hint of an idea as to where this might be leading, but he dismissed it, because he'd determinedly discounted it.

'Left or right?' Celeste prompted.

'Left.'

She pulled her hand from behind her back, and offered it to him but didn't reveal what was in it. 'Open it.'

Ben prised open her fingers and saw the little silver package, the key to heaven, and he was *so* tempted to reach out and take it.

'Celeste…'

'Before you say anything…' she laughed '…I didn't even know that I had them—I got a free bag of samples from the hospital, and I was looking for some nappy cream for Willow…' She didn't have to explain any more, so he smiled and interrupted her, reaching for her other hand and opening it to reveal the same contents.

'That's cheating,' Ben said.

'Why?'

'Because I can't lose.'

'Maybe you deserve to win.'

God, since Jen had died, sex had been just that—sex. Good, bad or indifferent, that was all it had ever been.

But with Celeste?

He stared into those amber eyes, his body charged with the memory of before and the possibility of after, her kiss still wet on his lips.

'I don't want to rush you,' he said gruffly.

'I *want* you to rush me,' she murmured back. How could she explain how different he made her feel? Sex had been a mystery for Celeste before Dean, yet how it had been for them was completely different from what she'd so far experienced with Ben. For her and Dean it had been a logical, preconceived act. Booking into a hotel on a Friday night, she had prepared for the occasion all week, nervousness mounting like the waxing moon and disappointment waning after the event.

But tonight, pressed into him, kissing him, ignoring

the film like two teenagers necking in a cinema, it had been the closest she had ever come to her body—to the bliss of a kiss and the intimacy of two people blocking out the world and letting someone else in.

It was neither logical nor preconceived.

And she certainly wasn't smooth and spraytanned!

But all it felt was right.

'You know I'm moving back home, Ben, so we won't be able to see each other that much, but just for tonight...'

'Are you sure?'

She was about to say something flip, but she stopped, looked into those lovely green eyes and there was no question—this was how it should have been, this was what it was all about, because this was Ben, and always, always, she'd wanted him. Now, finally, she could have him. That he wanted to forge some kind of a future with her—however that might turn out—just blew her mind.

'Absolutely,' Celeste said. 'Except...' She screwed her eyes closed.

'Say it,' he urged.

'I don't want to disappoint you.'

"You could *never* disappoint me,' he said emphatically.

'Oh.' She gave a very wry laugh. 'I might just surprise you.'

A mother she may be but she had little more sexual experience than an amoeba—and most of that had been gained tonight in Ben's living room.

He kissed her to the bedroom and beyond—only that didn't quell her nerves.

As Celeste dashed to the bathroom, Ben took a moment too...quickly turning over Jen's photo.

Celeste stood in front of the mirror, talking to herself and berating her lack of preparation for what was about to happen. Her bikini line stopped at all stations and as thin as she might be, thanks to Willow, bits of her wobbled in a way they never had before. Even if Ben assured her that he wasn't comparing her to his wife, Celeste was—imagining Jen's perfect white sports bras versus her rather faded maternity one.

She sighed heavily, girded her loins and went back into the bedroom, to where Ben was waiting for her. She jangled with nerves and cellulite for every second of the disrobing, torn between shame and want, but then Ben started kissing her again, hands stroking her, seemingly not fazed at all by her post-pregnancy body.

Rather liking it, in fact, Celeste soon realised. So why waste two hands covering yourself when there was six feet three of male pressed against you?

'We'll take it really slow...' he said, laying her down on the bed carefully. He lay down too, facing her, and then he kissed her. His legs without jeans were right up against hers—scratchy, big, muscly legs—and she was suddenly quivering with a mixture of excitement and fear, feeling as if she were about to turn over the page of an exam and hoping to hell she'd studied enough...

'What are you scared of?' he asked, quirking an eyebrow at her.

'I don't know,' she whispered back, closing her eyes once again.

Ben hated the man who had taken her confidence even before it had had the chance to bloom. Hated her self-doubts, but he had assurance enough for them both. But that she was scared of something so very, very wonderful saddened him too.

She was shaking with nerves as he took her in his arms. It felt so very different from before, because this time she knew where it was leading. He was so lovely to lie with, so big and male…and all hers. While they kissed she explored his body slowly, her hands running down his arms, feeling them solid and strong. Then she progressed to his chest—hard and flat and smooth. Her mouth moved there and she kissed the skin as his hands stroked and soothed her. Wrapped in this warm cocoon of skin and muscle and Ben, her hands slid over his hips and met solid thighs. She could feel him caressing her waist and over her hips, and it was Ben's mouth exploring her now, kissing her pale breasts, one hand moving to the front and making tiny circles on her soft stomach. Had there been a muscle working there, maybe she'd have thought about it and held it in, but there wasn't and anyway Celeste wasn't really thinking, her throat too tight with nerves as his hand crept downwards. Then he was stroking her and she made little noises, pretending to like it, but was too embarrassed to really. He kissed her again, so she stopped making all the right noises and kissed him back, concentrating on that, and tried not to resist his fingers slipping deep inside her, as his thumb stroked her softly and rhythmically.

She suddenly couldn't breathe, so she pulled in air and pulled it in again, and made the same sort of noise she'd been making before except now it came from a different place, this involuntary place that also made her sigh and moan and forget everything except Ben and how he was making her feel.

She held a man in her hand for the first time, exploring him, feeling him slide beneath her fingers, just touching and exploring, delighted with what she found. Ben was patient till he couldn't be patient any more. Her inexperience worried him, not for himself but for her— she was far too trusting and naïve—so he handed her the condom, which was something she should know how to do. But he ended up guiding her clumsy fingers as she rolled it down his length but, too eager, too nervous, she ripped it.

'We've only got one more!' she cried, embarrassed with her clumsiness. She wished he'd just do it for her, but Ben was insistent.

'I'll go to the petrol station if I have to and get some more if you rip this one,' he growled. God, he hoped he didn't have to! Practice may not make perfect, but a patient teacher helped and Celeste heard his moan of pleasure as she slipped it on slowly. Terrified of her nails, she unfurled it with her palms and then she was holding him lovingly for a moment, proud of her handiwork, as his fingers slipped deeper into her slippery warmth.

'I don't want to hurt you…' he gasped. He was suddenly right there at her entrance and she was tight with expectancy and fear. But then he was in just a little bit, two hands holding her hips and just gently stretching her till fear abated and she relaxed, willing him in further. But he was so supremely gentle, so strong and sure that there was pure bliss in there being no rush.

Always, in her vast repertoire of twice, there had

been an 'is that it?' moment. Is that what the world raves about? Is that all there is to it?

No, *this* was all there was to it.

All she wanted and all she wanted to be…

He was pushing her onto her back now, his huge frame moving over her, and it felt sublime…till she lost her rhythm and Ben dealt easily with that.

'Stay still.' His words were a low whisper in her ear.

'Still?' Wasn't she supposed to be writhing around? Surely lying still…

'Stay still,' he said again, so she did. She just lay and felt the blissful feel of him within her, the scent of him, of them, and she *really* did try to stay still, except her hips kept lifting, her body kept arching to his.

'Stay still…' he repeated, and she tried harder, except she couldn't, and suddenly she was lifting to him, moving with him, just locked in their own rhythm and Ben wasn't telling her any more because with that pause, she'd got it. Without trying hard, suddenly it was easy.

The skin of his chest was against her lips and she licked it, sucking his salty flesh, her legs around his, ankles trying to grip except he was so broad she could barely manage it. Then she felt the shift in him, something she'd never anticipated in the guarded, reticent Ben, because he was locked into this magical place too. There was no way she could define it, nothing specific with which to gauge it, except suddenly he was moaning her name and forgetting, deliciously forgetting to be gentle. Celeste was urging him on, not with words but with deep kisses on his chest and hands that slid over his buttocks and pushed him in harder. He was all over her, and so into her it made her dizzy, this full focus of him on her, until she was coming, a deep, deep orgasm that pleaded for him join her. And he did, giving in and just diving forward, shuddering his release and tipping Celeste to a place where there was no sound or silence or thought or want—just them and the beat of their bodies matching and minds colliding. She'd glimpsed pure magic and she never wanted to come down or go back or move from this place again.

He kissed her out of it, back to the world and then Ben rolled away from her and Celeste was suddenly scared, scared of losing whatever it was they had just found, scared of this place receding. Then it was her kissing him. On top of him, she kissed him hard, her hand threading into his hair, a silent plea for him not to leave her, for him not to retreat again inside himself because she had seen him now, seen *them* perhaps, glimpsed a marvellous possibility of them together, and she didn't want it to disappear.

CHAPTER TWELVE

'BEN RICHARDSON.'

She hadn't heard the phone ringing, just Ben's voice as he answered it. 'Belinda Hamilton is on call this weekend. No, I've seen her, she was there earlier tonight.' She felt the sheets move, Ben climb out, the shower taps on before the conversation was even over, and then two minutes later Ben, still dripping wet, was beside her, pulling on jeans. 'I've got to go into hospital for a bit.'

'Problem?'

'A bit—Belinda's not answering her pager.' He kissed her and it soothed her, but almost on cue, the moment he had gone, her three hours of sleep were up anyway, because Willow woke up. Celeste padded downstairs and prepared her a bottle, then brought her into bed to feed her. It was the easiest night feed Willow had ever taken, so blissfully easy. The bottle was gone in a few minutes and Willow was back asleep. She deserved a cuddle for being such a good girl, Celeste thought, and moved the pillows, cuddled her daughter in and determinedly ignored her mother's voice in her head that told her she shouldn't have the baby in bed with her.

And that was the scene Ben came home to.

Having dealt with the issue at work, he'd stopped at the petrol station, had bought *lots* of supplies and was ready to fall into bed. On the drive home it had all seemed straightforward, and Ben had felt so sure.

Then he'd called at Belinda's. Sure she was home, he had hammered on her door and felt this flicker of fear, the same fear he had when he'd come home to find Jen.

This silent house and the appalling feeling that something was wrong.

'Belinda!' he shouted. 'I'll call the police if you don't open up.'

'I'm sorry!' The door pulled open and he saw her eyes were swollen from crying. 'I just can't go in.'

'What's happened?' he asked, appalled.

'Can you just cover for me?' she whispered.

'Sure.'

'Can you ring the switchboard and tell them to page you if there's a problem?'

'I'll do it now,' Ben said, stopping the door as she went to close it. 'Belinda, what's going on?'

'Gastric flu…'

'Don't give me that!' he exclaimed.

'Please, Ben.'

It was none of his business. So long as she was okay, that was all that mattered, but his heart was still racing as he let himself into his home, the metallic taste of fear on his tongue and he downed a glass of water and then another before heading upstairs.

And then he'd seen them both on the bed, curled up like two kittens, sleeping, so sweet and perfect and innocent. But he'd glimpsed the past tonight, tasted fear again as he'd knocked at Belinda's door—and maybe that, Ben decided, was the sign he'd craved from Jen.

Maybe that was his warning.

Celeste stirred and half awoke, could see Ben sitting on the edge of the bed. 'How was it?'

'Busy enough, I just had to sort out some backlog, as they couldn't get hold of Belinda.'

'That's not like her,' Celeste frowned. 'Do you think she's okay?'

'She's fine,' Ben said. 'Well, not fine, as I stopped by her flat on the way back. She says she'd got gastric flu but my guess is…' He didn't finish. Belinda's personal life was her own and shouldn't really be gossiped about. 'It doesn't matter.'

Celeste knew she'd just been relegated, knew, though it was almost indefinable, that what she had feared—losing what she'd just found—had already taken place.

'I'll put Willow back in her pram.' She thought Ben might take the baby from her, but he didn't, so Celeste slipped out of bed and down to the guest room where she tucked her daughter into the pram. Then, as Willow woke up and started grumbling, she wheeled the stroller back to Ben's room and parked the baby in the corner as he undressed and climbed into bed.

It took a few moments to settle Willow and by the time she returned to his bed, Ben was asleep.

Or pretending to be.

She stared at his keys and the phone and the little paper bag from the garage, knowing what it contained and realising they wouldn't be needed.

Wondering what, in that short space of time, had changed things so much. She told herself she was imagining it—overreacting.

Maybe he *was* asleep after all and not just pretending.

The view from the bed was magical and it should have soothed her as she got into bed and lay next to him—only it didn't.

They'd agreed to take things slowly, dinners and dating—and the sex certainly hadn't been a problem. Even as inexperienced as she was, Celeste knew that for certain—what she had shared with Ben was so much more than she had ever expected or anticipated. So what had gone wrong between them?

Though cool and sophisticated wasn't really her forte, though she wanted to curl into him, to wake him with the kiss her body was demanding that she give, to roll over in the soft warm bed and feel his arms wrap around her, she resisted the temptation.

This was way too important to misjudge. So instead she slipped a reluctant body out of bed and checked on a still sleeping Willow, deciding to take advantage of the peace and have a shower, because if she'd stayed in bed she'd surely break the strained silence.

He lay still, hovering on the edge of the decision.

Ben knew that she was awake, knew she was waiting for him, knew that last night had confused her.

It had confused him too.

With Willow in the room, he hadn't slept a wink. It wasn't the little snuffles that kept him awake, it was the silences that killed him.

He walked across the room, checked that she was still breathing, which, of course, she was. In fact, as he looked down at her, she promptly opened her eyes and smiled at him.

Only Ben struggled to return it. Instead, he tried to go back to bed, but she'd seen him now and was starting to cry.

God, he hoped Celeste wouldn't be long in the shower.

Ben headed down stairs and made coffee for them both and a bottle for Willow, gritting his teeth as the cries grew louder, wondering if Celeste would be out of the shower by the time he got back up stairs.

Hoping so.

He walked back into the bedroom and put down the bottle and mugs, listened at the bathroom door and could still hear the shower—surely she could hear Willow crying?

Surely!

Ben stared into the stroller, picked up the baby's little soother and popped it in her mouth, but Willow spat it out in disgust, her eyes fixed on him, real tears at the edges, pleading with him to pick her up. So he tried, telling himself to pretend that he was at work where he operated on automatic, except this wasn't work.

He wanted to pick her up, even put his hands into the pram to do so…then he pulled back and tried rocking the pram instead, willing Celeste to come out of the shower and tend to her babe.

What the hell was he so scared of?

Cross with himself, Ben paced the room. He would just go right over and pick her up and be done with it.

Then he heard the bleep of Celeste's phone.

Dean

He didn't read the text—just felt the chill of a shadow, a big black bird in the sky that could swoop down and take them at any given moment…

'Willow!' Shivering wet, wrapped in a towel, Celeste headed straight for the pram, scooping her daughter up in her arms, feeling her hot, red face and turning questioning eyes to him. 'She's been sobbing!'

'I was about to knock and tell you,' he said lamely.

'To knock?' Celeste stared at him open-mouthed. 'Did you not think to pick her up?'

'I was making coffee,' Ben said defensively. 'And her bottle.'

Which sounded logical and reasonable, Celeste realised—except babies were neither logical nor reasonable, and Willow had needed to be held.

'Can you hold her for me?' Celeste's voice held just a hint of challenge. 'I just need to get dressed…'

'I have to shower and get dressed too,' Ben lied. 'Switch just called, I have to go into work.'

'Ben…' For someone usually so emotional, Celeste's voice was ominously calm. 'I'm not asking you to feed her or change her, I'm asking if you could hold Willow for two minutes.'

'Sorry.' He shook his head. 'I've got to get ready.'

'Ben?' She couldn't believe it, couldn't believe the way he was acting. 'I'm not asking for—'

'Look,' Ben interrupted, 'she's not my…' He didn't finish, his mouth snapping closed before this morning turned into the mother of all mornings, but Celeste finished for him.

'Not your *problem*?' That wasn't what he'd been about to say, but it was easier to nod than to explain. 'God.' Celeste gave a mirthless laugh. 'I really know how to pick jerks, don't I?'

Ben didn't answer so she spoke instead.

'Just how *slowly* did you want to take it, Ben? What, by the time she went to school, maybe we could move in with you?' she said scathingly.

'Willow's father just texted….'

'Don't blame this on him!' Celeste retorted. 'You've been off with me since last night.' When he didn't answer that, she asked again, 'Just how slowly did you mean, Ben?'

'I don't know.'

She stared down at her daughter, *the* most important person in the world to her, and she knew what she had to do.

'I'm not putting her through this.' Willow was starting to whimper. Her mother's arms were a nice place, but it would be even better with a bottle. 'I should have listened from the start—you don't want kids and I've got one.'

Her phone bleeped again and Celeste gritted her teeth. What the hell did Dean want?

'You'd better see what her father wants!' Ben was done. She was right, Willow deserved better than him, and the only way out was to end it—really end it. 'After all, she's his responsibility.'

'Correction!' Celeste spat, hating him too much at this moment for tears. 'She's *mine.*'

He didn't respond, just headed for the shower.

'You might be glad to get rid of me and Willow, Ben,' she called to his departing back. 'But you've no idea what you just lost.' He closed the door behind him and knew, because he knew Celeste, that she'd be gone when he came out, that she wouldn't hang around to debate the point. He turned on the shower full blast, and prayed she'd go soon, because while the water might drown the sound of Willow's tears, it wouldn't drown his.

It wasn't Willow that was his problem.

He sat on the floor of the shower and held his head in his hands.

It was his own daughter.

It was a hurt like she'd never known.

A rejection not just of her—that she could deal with, had dealt with in the past and could deal with again now. It was the rejection of Willow that was as acute as a sting but didn't abate like one.

Was this the price of motherhood—that the man of her dreams could walk away from her so easily?

Well, let him.

'How long will you be?' Her mother hovered at the door, holding Willow.

'I don't know,' Celeste snapped. After weeks of nagging for Celeste to speak with Willow's father, now that the moment was here, her mother was demanding timelines! Did she not realise how hard this was? 'There are bottles made up.'

'You will be coming back to get Willow, won't you?'

That didn't even deserve an answer, so Celeste just gritted her teeth.

'Maybe you should take her with you…'

'Mum!' It wasn't a snap this time, just a plea for her to stop fretting, worrying, fixing… And then Celeste got it, answered the question that she had wrestled with for weeks, no, for months now. Seven weeks into motherhood and Celeste was starting to get the swing of it—this aching, endless worry lasted longer than the pregnancy, longer than the first days or months. She was stuck with this fear for her child for life—as was her own mum—and now when her voice came, it was gentler, more reasonable, friendly even. 'I'm not going to parade Willow in front of him—he hasn't even asked to see her. I'm just going to see what he wants.'

'What do *you* want?'

'I don't know,' Celeste admitted. 'For some sort of father for Willow, I suppose…'

'What if he wants you back?' It was the first real conversation they'd had in years and Celeste was finally able to answer honestly.

'He lost me a long time ago, Mum. I'm only meeting with him now for the sake of Willow.'

'Be careful,' Rita said, and Celeste nodded.

'Don't wor—' The words died on her lips and then Celeste smiled. 'Okay, worry away if you must, but you really don't have to. Whatever he has to say, Willow and I are going to be fine.'

Seeing him again, all Celeste felt was older and maybe, possibly, just a little bit wiser.

There was none of that giddy rush she'd had as a student when he'd walked into the lecture room—no blushing when he spoke or hanging on to his every word.

Whether she'd wanted to or not, she'd well and truly grown up and could see Dean for what he was now—a rather sad attempt of a man who'd played on her naïvety, who had taken full advantage of a perfectly normal crush when he *really* should have known better.

The rules were there for a reason.

It was a very short meeting, and not at all sweet. He wanted assurances that his perfect life wasn't about to end soon, that Celeste wasn't suddenly going to change her mind and come knocking—an assurance she was only too happy to provide!

'What will you tell Willow?' he asked diffidently.

'The truth.' Celeste looked at him coolly. 'Probably a nicer version of it. I'll miss out the bit where you offered to pay for an abortion—but she'll grow up with the truth. And when she's old enough, what she does with that truth will be her decision, Dean.'

Then there was nothing else to say, nothing at all, so she didn't bother. Just stood up and walked out of the café and took a big breath and then another one.

Until finally she blew the last one out and let him go.

Then Celeste put one foot in front of the other and did it again, just kept on putting one foot in front of the other, which meant she was walking.

Walking away and getting on with the rest of her life.

CHAPTER THIRTEEN

'WHAT'S going on, Belinda?' It took till five on Monday to talk to Belinda. All day she'd been avoiding him and, clearly thinking he'd already gone home, she walked into the office and did an about-turn, but Ben halted her.

'Nothing.'

'I need to know why you didn't answer your pager on Friday night.'

'I'm sorry about that. I honestly felt so unwell, I just…'

'Belinda, I covered for you, but I'm not going to be fobbed off,' he warned.

'He's still married.' Belinda crumpled as she admitted it. 'I found out on Saturday night…that multi-trauma…'

Ben frowned.

'It was his son.'

'Oh, Belinda.'

'I rang his number but ended up speaking to his wife…I recognised the surname, then she called him to the phone…' She could barely get the words out for crying. 'I just couldn't stay in the department and see him, face her. You think I'd be used to it by now…'

'Used to what?'

'Being let down.' He could scarcely believe the change in her from the confident, outgoing woman he'd first met. 'I'm so embarrassed.'

'Embarrassed?' he asked, bewildered.

'I just feel like a fool,' Belinda admitted. 'I knew he was busy, I made so many excuses for him—he was at work, or with the kids… I guess I just gave him a million and one reasons to justify why he could only give me such a little bit of his time.'

'It's not your fault,' Ben said, and it wasn't Celeste's fault either—if the stunning, streetwise Belinda could be taken in, what chance had Celeste had? 'You were just…' he gave an uncomfortable shrug as analysing emotions was not his strongest point '…trying to be happy…'

'Like we all are,' Belinda said. 'Only we just end up hurting a whole lot of people along the way.' She took a gulp of her coffee. 'I feel such a fool,' she said again despairingly.

'*He's* the fool,' Ben insisted.

'That's not how it feels from here.' She gave a watery smile. 'I'll be okay… I just need to lie low for a bit, lick my wounds…'

'I can imagine.'

'But I'll get there.' Belinda blew out a breath. 'Get back out there soon…'

Ben realised he would never understand some people—never get how someone who had been so hurt could, in such a short time, be talking about getting back out there, laying their hearts on the line, only to have them broken again.

Why?

Except he suspected he was starting to know the answer. It was he who was the fool—he worked that one out as he drove home that evening.

There were all these people out there, searching for happiness, trying not to be lonely, and he'd had it right there, not once, but twice, *right there* for the taking.

He'd just been too scared of getting hurt again to move on and take what was on offer.

He had wanted a world that came with iron-clad guarantees—and because that was impossible, well, he'd stepped right off the planet. Made some half-hearted attempt to move on with his life—only by *his* safe rules. He'd rather have sex than a relationship, and the more meaningless the better, because then you didn't get hurt. And no children or feelings involved either, please, because that could hurt too. As could biological fathers that might pop up…

Only being lonely hurt more than the risk of loving.

And now he'd lost her too.

He got stuck in his street as a small rental truck pulled out of the units—his big black bird swooping down and taking her away. He could see her car in her drive and knew she was inside her flat, organising the moving of her stuff over to her parents' house in preparation for the coming weekend. If she went to live with her parents, he knew he had lost her for ever.

He finally realised that this was his moment.

That *this* moment was all anyone had.

And he had to start living in it. He took a deep breath and headed for her door.

* * *

'It's not a good time, Ben.'

He could hear Willow's cries as she went to close the door on him.

'I need to talk to you.'

'And *I* need to feed my baby!' She opened the door, her face angry. 'So I hope you can stomach being in the same room as her as you say whatever it is that you have to.'

Willow's screams were louder and louder as they walked through her tiny unit. Everything that was them was gone—the crib, the flowers, the throw rugs, the ironing board by the wall. Just the drab furniture remained and as he followed her through the place, the kitchen was empty, except for a kettle and a jug and a bottle warming.

'It's coming, Willow…' He could hear the strain in her voice as she tried to keep it light for her baby. 'The microwave's gone with the removal…' He watched as she tested the bottle on her wrist then placed it back in the water, and then she snapped, 'I'm just going to feed her and then I'll be gone. I've decided to go before the weekend. There's no point hanging around now.'

'Don't go.'

'Just what the hell do you want, Ben?' she asked wearily.

'You.'

'Well, sorry, but I'm already taken…' Even though she was in the lounge, Celeste had to shout over Willow's screams. 'And I wouldn't have it any other way.'

'I don't *want* it any other way,' he said desperately.

'She isn't going to go away, Ben. I'm not going to

pretend she doesn't exist so we can sleep together a couple of times a week!'

'I want Willow too…' She had no idea how hard that was for him to say, no idea of the terror of that admission, so she scorned him instead.

'Oh, so you'll *tolerate* her so you can have her mother.'

'No, I'll try harder. I want her too,' he said again.

'Just leave it, Ben!'

'Jen was pregnant when she died.' Real pain demanded respect. Real pain could be felt and heard and acknowledged, even if we don't know how, because even Willow fell silent. 'About the same stage as you when you had Willow.'

'You should have told me,' Celeste said, shocked.

'How?' Ben shook his head. 'It's not something you just slip into the conversation—and especially being pregnant yourself…' he gave a thin smile '…you didn't need to hear it.'

'No.' She admitted the truth of that. She'd been struggling enough as it was.

'I wanted to tell you after you had Willow…but…I lost my baby, Celeste, and I couldn't do it to you. Give you that fear that you might lose yours too.'

'How?'

'A subarachnoid haemorrhage. Just like that.' He clapped his hands and it made her jump, but it seemed appropriate. She'd learnt about them at uni—a sudden, severe, thunderclap headache—and she felt like crying except it wasn't her place to right now. 'I came home and found her…' And then he corrected himself, because it wasn't really Jen that was the problem, he had loved and lost her and would miss her for ever, but in that he had moved on—had almost reached that place of acceptance, just not quite. 'No, I came home and found *them*.

'She was buried inside Jen and I never got to hold her and I never really got to mourn her—and I don't know how to start.'

'You just did.'

He nodded, screwed his eyes closed and pressed his fingers against them as, dizzy with images, like a roundabout, he willed it to stop.

'Tell me,' she implored.

'I can't go there,' he said, because he truly couldn't. 'I didn't want to love you, but I do, Celeste, and I don't want to love Willow, but I know I will. I'm so scared of losing you…'

'You did, though, Ben.' She was still angry, so angry with him. 'You don't want to fall in love in case something happens, so you'd rather just let us go…'

'I'm here now.'

'Half of you!' Celeste exclaimed. 'And the other half is stuck in a place where no one can visit. Well, Willow and I deserve more than that.'

'I'll give you more than that,' he vowed.

'When?' Celeste demanded, and Ben couldn't believe his ears.

'What are you asking for, Celeste?'

'Your love,' Celeste said, and her heart was breaking, but she was determined to be very, very strong.

'I just did. I told you I love you…'

'No, Ben.'

'And I *will* love Willow.'

'No.' She absolutely meant it.

'I don't know what you want here, Celeste!' It was Ben that was angry now—he'd never been more open, more honest, had never revealed his heart like this since Jen died, and now he knew why. 'What? Do you want me to say that I love Willow?'

'Anyone can *say* it,' she pointed out.

'Okay?' He picked up the bottle. 'Am I to hold her, to feed her?'

'I'm quite capable of that.'

'What, then?' Ben demanded, because he didn't know what she wanted from him, didn't know what test she had in her mind that he had to pass.

'I want you to *let* yourself love her.' All she did was confuse him, because he *was* going to love her, in time, he knew that it would grow. 'And when you do, we'll both be here waiting for you…'

'I don't understand you, Celeste.'

'Well, *I* don't understand *you*.' She picked up the bottle and walked into the lounge and picked up Willow, feeding her in silence as he stood at the door and watched.

'You can't just demand instant love,' he protested.

'I can,' Celeste came back immediately. 'She's already got one poor excuse for a father—she doesn't need another, hanging around, waiting for love to grow.'

'You're impossible!' he growled.

'I'm very straightforward, actually,' she replied calmly.

'Say goodbye to Ben.' She stood up, held up a little hand and waved it at him. 'We'll see him when he's ready.'

She put Willow in her crib and tucked her in. 'Now, if you'll excuse me, I need to get on with my packing.'

'That's it?' he asked incredulously.

'That's it,' she confirmed.

'I've come over here, I've told you why, I've told you I love you and that I'll do everything I can for Willow, and it's not enough?' He walked over and looked her in the eyes. 'It's not enough for you?'

'No.'

She meant it, he knew that she meant it, he just didn't get it. 'I don't understand you, Celeste,' he said again helplessly, and kissed her on her taut cheek. 'I'll go.'

'Please.'

'I'll *never* understand your mother,' he said, looking at Willow. He stroked her little cheek and again it was Willow who looked into his eyes—the same way she had the day she'd been born and the next morning too.

Once more, Ben closed his eyes, only this time he opened them again, and she was still there, smiling—patiently waiting for him to love her.

He didn't want to do this—he felt as if he were dying—in fact, he was sure it would have been easier *to* have died.

'She was made for you, Ben,' Celeste said softly beside him, staring down at her daughter and understanding the world now. 'Because you'd never have done this yourself—you'd never have done it again.'

She was right—and somewhere deep inside him something aligned. Because even with Celeste, without a certain little lady being born into his hands, under his tree, he would never have taken that chance again, would never, ever have risked having another baby.

Yet he risked it now.

He looked at this little new life and remembered all that hope, all that love, all that promise he'd once had…

'She was never born.' It probably didn't make sense to Celeste, yet it was so vital to him. He could feel the petal of Willow's cheek as soft and white as a daisy and it felt as if he was being hollowed out inside. He still wanted to run, only there was no beach long enough, no universe that could contain the grief that split him. 'There's no birth certificate, and we hadn't chosen a name…' It hadn't felt right to name her without Jen.

He could never separate the two, had grieved for Jen and their baby, but had never actually separated them, had never let himself grieve just for the baby. 'She was never born.'

'She still *was*, though,' Celeste said, her voice there beside him, her arm around him—and if he'd been there for her before, she was there for him now. 'She still *is*.'

'Daisy.'

He stroked Willow's cheek and finally named the daughter he should have had. And just as he had cut Willow's cord, Willow let him cut his daughter's—her little star hands holding his as grief pitted him. In holding Willow he got to hold his own baby, pressed his lips to her soft cheeks, got to hold Daisy just for a moment, and then sent her back to rest with her mum.

'I love you.' He said it to Willow who was there now, only he didn't just say it, he felt it too. He held her close, but he didn't just hold her—he finally let himself love her, finally let himself hope, and he promised her silently that he would always be there for her. 'And I love your mum too.'

'She knows that,' Celeste said.

'Don't go to your parents'.' Holding her baby, he turned to Celeste. 'Come home.'

And it was home—even if she'd never lived there, his house was already her home.

'Well, I'm all packed.' She was smiling and crying, so very, very proud—and safe too—and for the first time in the longest time absolutely sure. 'I'd better ring Mum and tell her. She'll be on her way soon.'

'What will she say?'

'She'll probably be relieved.' Celeste laughed. 'I'm not the easiest person to live with.'

'I can't wait to find out,' he murmured.

He didn't want her, didn't want them in this shabby, bare unit a moment longer. He wanted them home where they all belonged. The boxes and crib and bags and baby baths and car could all wait till later, so Celeste rang Rita and Ben packed a quick bag for Willow, and they walked down the street pushing a pram, only as a family this time. She was *such* a good baby, because she slept for a couple of very necessary hours while Ben and Celeste kissed and made up and cried a bit too, and when Celeste finally fell asleep in his arms, Ben stayed awake, just so he could feel her warm skin. Then he heard Willow, who was starting to stir in her pram, and he finally felt what had been missing for all those years.

Peace.

A peace that wasn't shattered by Willow's lusty cries, a peace that remained as Celeste chatted incessantly on as she brought in the baby's bottle and then handed him an angry bundle as she decided that instead of feeding her daughter, *he* could do it while she explored the spa in her new bathroom!

Peace as, fed, changed and content, he put Willow back in the pram and wound up her mobile for her.

Peace perfect peace, Celeste thought as she lay in the spa, her toes wrinkling, knowing how much he loved the two of them, mother and daughter. She stared out at the glorious view and at a wonderful future too.

'Marry me!' Celeste shouted to the silence.

'I was about to suggest the same thing,' Ben said, standing in the doorway grinning. 'We should get married out there on the beach, where we met…'

'I take it that's a yes?'

'It's a yes…' He looked out to the beach and he could almost see them—see their wedding, Celeste holding Willow, the celebrant, with family and friends gathered around, and he could almost see Jen, holding Daisy and smiling. And it was a blessing, a long-awaited blessing, to be able to think of them both and smile.

'Oh, well, if you insist.' She laughed.

Lost in thought, he had no idea what she was talking about. 'Pardon?'

'I suppose there's no talking you out of it…' She gave a martyred sigh. 'I guess you'd better climb in and ravish me.'

He didn't ever compare, because there was no comparison—two more different women he could never imagine, and yet he loved them both. But it was then, when he least expected it, that he got his sign, the one he had been longing for from Jen, because just for a second he could have sworn he heard Jen laugh, could have sworn he heard her letting him go with grace, urging him on, to live this wonderful life.

And Ben laughed too.

Laughed as he climbed right in to join Celeste to do as the grad nurse ordered.

Ravish her.

EPILOGUE

NEVER, not once, did she wonder or doubt.

Not even a little bit.

Despite her mother's gloomy predictions, despite what she'd read in the 'blended family' section of a baby book, which Celeste had finally thrown against the wall—not once did she think that their baby would change how he felt about Willow.

Because without Willow, there would be no them.

'It won't be long now.' Ben squeezed her shoulder as she lay on the operating table—with all the passion of a doctor to a patient, but that was what he did sometimes.

They'd experienced three pregnancies between them and all of them had been different.

This had been a textbook pregnancy (if you excluded her massive weight gain), and had gone brilliantly till the very last minute—but eight hours of huffing and puffing and still their baby wouldn't come out!

She'd worked part time till seven months, because that was what she did.

She had told him about her backache and sore ankles

but had spoken to the obstetrician, rather than him, when she'd had a ripper of a headache.

And he'd massaged her tummy and kissed her bump and done all the right things throughout.

They both had.

Jollied each other along and assured the other it would be fine.

'I'm scared…' She wasn't even sedated—they had been so mean with drugs that she was thinking of writing a letter of complaint. So much for being a doctor's wife! An epidural might numb your stomach, but it didn't numb your brain.

'What if it changes things?'

No matter how neatly folded, no matter where it was stored, your baggage came on the journey with you—and every now and then you had to cough up and pay the excess or watch as Customs ripped open the zipper and demanded to know what a chocolate bar was doing hidden in your bra.

As if you could explain how it got there.

As if you had meant to pack it and haul it to the other side of the world.

Except you had.

'I don't want it to change anything,' she wailed.

'Change can be good,' he said reassuringly.

It was only the three of them, her and him and Willow. And she was scared for them, scared for the coming baby—scared of change. Only it was happening, whether she wanted it to or not.

'I'm scared, Ben,' she said again.

'I know.'

She could see tears swimming in his green eyes.

'Remember Willow—she was so floppy and ill…'

'And look at her now.'

She knew they were making the incision because the OB had told her, but she only had eyes for Ben.

Could hear the gurgle as they suctioned her waters and she was petrified.

'How can I love it as much as Willow?'

'Wait and see,' he suggested gently.

It was a him.

This beefy whopper of a boy that they held up over the drapes, with a flat nose and bunched-up forehead, who screamed and cried and kicked all the way to the little cot set up for him.

'No wonder I needed a Caesarean.' She just had to smile, had to cry, had to gaze in wonder.

And, of course, so did Ben.

He walked over and stared at his son, got the footprints on his T-shirt and then came back to Celeste.

'You should see the *size* of him!' he said in awe.

'Now do you see why I moaned when he kicked?' she gasped.

She got a quick kiss when they brought him over all wrapped up—but so was she, so she couldn't really touch him. But there were too many people around for real tears.

'Go with him…' Celeste said to her husband.

It was all a blur from there. They were a bit more generous with drugs, and she was stitched and sent to Recovery and then to her room. And Celeste sort of remembered her mum coming and Ben's mum too and a lot of noise…

And later, much later, she woke up.

And remembered.

She wasn't scared of Ben's feelings, not even a tiny bit, okay maybe, just maybe a smudge…

But he had his back to her and his son and a fretful one-year-old on his hip who he was showing the moon to, and that left her alone to stare at her new baby.

She was scared of her *own* feelings.

He was so little.

A huge baby, but really so little and new and wrinkly and perfect, and she was so scared she wouldn't get this right. Then he opened his eyes…

Just stared right at her and demanded she love him.

She would very soon, except she was really tired. 'Ashley…'

She was too sore to pick him up, so Ben did it for her, balancing Willow on one side as he scooped up his son and handed him to her.

'It means "from the ashes",' Celeste said. 'I looked it up.'

'I bet you did.'

'Baby!' Willow forgot for a moment how tired she was. Delighted with both her *finally* awake brother and her vocal skills, she'd recently discovered chanting. 'Baby, baby, baby!' And she clambered over the bed and a catheter, coming dangerously close to a Caesarean incision, and then smothered her brother with kisses and germs followed by lots more gooey kisses.

Then Ashley got a kiss from Dad.

And then Celeste got a kiss from a suddenly very needy, tearful Willow.

There was almost too much love to go around, Celeste thought, very near tears herself.

'I'm going to get her home,' Ben told her.

He'd seen her watery eyes and he understood.

Knew when she needed him, even when she didn't admit it.

And knew when she needed to be on her own too.

The midwives walked in on his kiss to Celeste, but that was okay, because there would be lots of kisses later—she needed wise women with her now.

Tonight was for Celeste to meet Ash.

Ben understood that.

Tonight was the time for Celeste to discover that there was plenty of her to go around.

'Push the button…' He stepped in the lift and guided Willow's hand to the 'G' button—but she managed to miss and they headed for the roof instead!

'You're as unpredictable as your mother!' he huffed.

'Daddy!' She'd said it so many times, but she said it again—started up her chant and continued it all the way to the car park where he strapped her in and drove her home. 'Daddy, Daddy, Daddy!'

He was hers and she was his and never let anyone say otherwise.

He made her milk, put Willow in her cot, kissed her goodnight and turned on her mobile.

Then rang uncles and cousins and friends and deleted the text he wanted to send to Celeste in case it disturbed her sleep—he'd tell her himself in the morning.

Then he checked in on Willow and changed his mind and sent the text anyway.

Willow sound asleep—give ash a kiss—i love you.

And amid a frustrating attempt at a feed with an angry, hungry baby, and with nipples that hurt, a midwife smiled and handed her the phone. Celeste read her text, but didn't reply. He already knew she loved him too, so she just did as instructed. She leant forward and placed her lips on an angry forehead, erased crinkles with soft lips, felt the melting in her heart as Ash snuffled towards her and, after just a beat of a pause, Celeste resumed trusting again.

Felt the sweet weight of a new baby in her arms—and wanted it, could do it, was doing it right now…

It really *was* that simple.

Love grew if you let it.

MEDICAL™ 2-in-1

Coming next month

THE DOCTOR'S LOST-AND-FOUND BRIDE
by Kate Hardy

The devastating loss of their baby blew Marina and Max's young marriage apart. Years later, thrown together by work, they're shocked to find their incredible spark is still burning! But is it enough to mend the marriage they've always wanted?

MIRACLE: MARRIAGE REUNITED
by Anne Fraser

Niall and Robina once had a marriage in a million. But the cracks are showing as Robina aches for the baby she fears she can never have… They must find a way to harness their love and fight for a future – together.

A MOTHER FOR MATILDA
by Amy Andrews

Paramedic Lawson, a devoted single dad, knows he can only see colleague Victoria as his work partner. Until Victoria decides to leave, and Lawson's emotions are sent into freefall! Can Lawson persuade Victoria to stay for his little girl…and for him?

THE BOSS AND NURSE ALBRIGHT
by Lynne Marshall

Brooding doctor Jason meets his match in forthright nurse Claire Albright… And her little girl, Gina, reminds Jason of the daughter he lost. Can Claire and Gina do the unimaginable – make Jason smile again and be part of their happy family?

On sale 5th March 2010

MEDICAL™

Single titles coming next month

NEW SURGEON AT ASHVALE A&E
by Joanna Neil

Dr Ruby Martyn swaps her white coat for wellies and a pram, leaving her job at Ashvale to care for her adorable niece. But the A&E can't cope without her and neither can her boss, gorgeous doctor Sam! Convincing Ruby to return is important, but first on his agenda is winning her heart!

DESERT KING, DOCTOR DADDY
by Meredith Webber

Sheikh Yusef knows his kingdom will benefit from doctor Gemma's renowned approach to medicine, and the immediate connection between beautiful Gemma and his tiny daughter amazes him! As a man *and* a father, he knows what he must do: this sheikh surgeon will make Gemma his royal bride!

On sale 5th March 2010

millsandboon.co.uk Community

Join Us!

The Community is the perfect place to meet and chat to kindred spirits who love books and reading as much as you do, but it's also the place to:

- ■ Get the inside scoop from authors about their latest books
- ■ Learn how to write a romance book with advice from our editors
- ■ Help us to continue publishing the best in women's fiction
- ■ Share your thoughts on the books we publish
- ■ Befriend other users

Forums: Interact with each other as well as authors, editors and a whole host of other users worldwide.

Blogs: Every registered community member has their own blog to tell the world what they're up to and what's on their mind.

Book Challenge: We're aiming to read 5,000 books and have joined forces with The Reading Agency in our inaugural Book Challenge.

Profile Page: Showcase yourself and keep a record of your recent community activity.

Social Networking: We've added buttons at the end of every post to share via digg, Facebook, Google, Yahoo, technorati and de.licio.us.

www.millsandboon.co.uk

2 FREE BOOKS
AND A SURPRISE GIFT

We would like to take this opportunity to thank you for reading this Mills & Boon® book by offering you the chance to take TWO more specially selected books from the Medical™ series absolutely FREE! We're also making this offer to introduce you to the benefits of the Mills & Boon® Book Club™—

- **FREE home delivery**
- **FREE gifts and competitions**
- **FREE monthly Newsletter**
- **Exclusive Mills & Boon Book Club offers**
- **Books available before they're in the shops**

Accepting these FREE books and gift places you under no obligation to buy, you may cancel at any time, even after receiving your free books. Simply complete your details below and return the entire page to the address below. You don't even need a stamp!

YES Please send me 2 free Medical books and a surprise gift. I understand that unless you hear from me, I will receive 5 superb new stories every month including two 2-in-1 books priced at £4.99 each and a single book priced at £3.19, postage and packing free. I am under no obligation to purchase any books and may cancel my subscription at any time. The free books and gift will be mine to keep in any case.

Ms/Mrs/Miss/Mr _____ Initials _____

Surname _____

Address _____

_____

_____ Postcode _____

Send this whole page to: Mills & Boon Book Club, Free Book Offer, FREEPOST NAT 10298, Richmond, TW9 1BR